ORLA RAFFERTY SEEKS HER FORTUNE

ORLA RAFFERTY SEEKS HER FORTUNE

Margaret Pinard

Chapter 1

Orla folded the crisp black fabric several times before it consented to fit into the clothes press where her full mourning clothes would now live. The black was still crisp, she reflected, because she hadn't gone out in the sun much in her year of adjustment to widowhood. No, she had not been out of doors much, even when the weather was fine. Not that fine weather occurred often in her patch of southwest Scotland.

She sported a violet gown now: she'd had it made up in March when it was still quite chilly, and it was up to the challenge of Crookston's April gales. The year of adjustments had been necessary, as not only was Orla accustoming herself to a life alone after fourteen years with her husband, but she was also acclimating her mind to the idea of living independently.

While she hadn't gone out in the sun often, she had gone to the village celebrations and to dinners when she was invited; her grief was not so taxing that she take to her bed like one of the Romantic heroines of the novels she read. Their marriage had been quiet and unassuming, comfortable. The village understood that. She rather thought they considered her practical and unsentimental. Still, these limited social encounters during her mourning had pointed to the most awkward part of the transition she would now face as a widow: what was her role?

Should she recommend a name for the curacy that was now open? She might be asked for her opinion by the minister who had replaced her husband, or she might not. What would be expected of her in giving alms? She had always been the rector's wife, and gone to the aid of parishioners as was her role, but now, who would come to her for help? She had been left comfortably off, with her own cottage—but they wouldn't know her income. They wouldn't know how she fit in with the community now, exactly. Would she be pitied? Should she show her hand?

And what hand did she have, in fact? A letter had been delivered this April morning of 1833, bearing her name and a London return. She was glad to see that the letters to her husband had finally stopped. But this was likely to be from their solicitor, the only person she could think of in London who might have business with her. Robert had moved several times for the Church, and so had preferred to keep a London solicitor for his affairs. Very inconvenient it had made the reading of the will and disposition of his effects. But what could he be writing to her about now?

She smoothed the envelope once more and put it aside. It could wait til after her visit to Isobel.

The adjustments had been coming all her life: first, as a poor Irish emigrant's daughter; then as a servant in the Manse; then marrying the kind, visiting curate, and finally, losing him to a sudden illness. Orla knew a visit to her cranky father would be due soon, but she wanted to see a friendly face first.

Her friend Isobel had been a widow longer than she. She did not know of Orla's roots in the emigrant community, nor of her years of servitude and late conversion to the Episcopalian faith. Isobel was happy to talk of light subjects, local gossip, and the frivolous, repetitive tasks that took up her days. Sometimes Orla preferred to visit the sisters Arbischer, one a spinster, one a widow, who lived together and were much more reserved and serious. But today, Orla's whim took her to her bright friend's door at the other end of Crookston. Her knock brought the single maid to the door. Jenny smiled a welcome and stepped back to allow her to pass through.

"Good morning, Mrs. Smith. Mrs. Foxton was just talking of your call."

"Was she? How did she know?" Orla gave her an amused smile as she handed over her well-worn cape.

"Mrs. Foxton wagered this as your anniversary. Said you'd be wanting to be out with the new half-mourning gown. It do look lovely, ma'am."

"Thank you, Jenny. Mrs. Foxton does indeed know me well. Is she in the parlor?"

"Yes, ma'am."

Orla nodded and turned down the small hallway to the parlor. Isobel's circumstances had been thoroughly discussed, as a practical subject, many times before, and Orla had already partially disclosed her new situation. She had to ask her not to bandy it about, since she knew Isobel would not consider it necessary to hide a friend's good fortune from all and sundry. She knew her friend's strengths as well as her foibles.

The door to the parlor was open, but Orla tapped on it all the same.

"Oh, I knew it would be you! Come in, do sit down, my dear. Let us have a look at the new gown first."

Isobel was seated on the side of the settee nearest the window. Orla tried to summon some gracefulness as she walked in slowly and twirled in front of the settee.

"Ravishing, my dear. Quite a good eye your seamstress has for detail. Though you know I swear by my Minnie."

"I do," Orla said ruefully, but with a smile. If she'd heard Isobel sing Minnie's praises once, she'd heard it a thousand times over the years they'd been acquaintances. She sat on one of the two chairs facing the settee. It wasn't a large room but it was comfortably furnished and had a good fire going. Her hostess made sure to have everything in good order and good taste, at whatever level she could afford. Orla was less bothered about those things.

"And I know I'm not 'ravishing' to anyone at this age, Isobel, but it's kind of you to say so. She did do a clever job with the wrap collar to the waistband, and I do love the pattern of muslins she put into the bib—I could never have had the imagination."

"Well, then, tell us what your imagination has been up to! Are you feeling a bit stronger, more sorted out in general?" She gave Orla a critical perusal, which made her want to clench her teeth. Instead she exhaled slowly. *Light topics, friendly face,* she thought. *This will help prepare me to beard the lion in its den,* she thought, meaning her father.

"Thank you for remembering the date, Isobel. It is very thoughtful of you."

"Of course, my dear. We all have our little mountains to climb. I wanted to be sure to be on hand for yours." She smiled and tilted her head, waiting.

"There's no great announcement coming, you needn't worry. Besides the wardrobe changes, I will be back about my usual routines. I intend to write to my friends in Hampshire and in Northumberland to go up and have a stay with them, so I shall have the little excitement of a tour round the country, come summer."

"Oh, that's marvelous! These are the Darcys and the Burches you've visited before?"

"Yes, just the ones. They are kind and generous to me these years."

"Of course, why shouldn't they be? Sometimes I wish I lived farther away so you could visit me for a house party." Isobel grinned. "But do you know, there is some local excitement I shall be keen on observing while you are away… I'm sure you haven't yet heard, keeping at home as you have been."

Orla shook her head, inviting her to continue.

"You know we only have one family of note in the parish, the Shaws, but they have had a guest this past week who, it appears, intends to purchase a nearby estate."

The excitement in the woman's voice—Orla suppressed a groan. Matchmaking was the one of Isobel's hobbies that Orla liked least. She wondered briefly if she could yet steer the conversation to the other dresses she'd ordered, but no, Isobel had her bone and would gnaw at it.

"His family have a fine townhouse in Glasgow. Yes, not Edinburgh, sadly, but they are quite rich. His father owns an import firm with a viscount—an actual Peer! And they say he is come to our neighborhood to find a good bit of property and," she paused dramatically, "a wife."

"Is that so?" Orla replied neutrally. "And who is the 'they' who 'say,' pray?"

The brief smile at her rhyme disappeared as the excited woman continued.

"Oh, you know," she said breezily. "The farmers' wives at the church and parson himself, I believe." She lowered her head and cocked an eyebrow at Orla. "But I don't suppose you're ready yet."

Orla cast her gaze down, shaking her head slightly. She was still laying plans for her adjustments, still trying to embody that self-possessed widow that she had seen Isobel project for the past several years.

"Well, I certainly am. Interested in the possibility, anyway," said her friend. "I am growing weary of our friendly backwater, my dear, it must be said."

"How can you say that, when only last week we had a special delivery of newest satin at the haberdasher's and a barrow-man on the same day selling the new royal pattern of porcelain?" She kept her face innocent.

Isobel didn't even bother with a prim reprimand, just gave one of her arch looks that made Orla laugh.

Chapter 2

Orla was in charity with the world as she swept back into her cottage that evening. The visit with Isobel had done her good, and the anniversary was settling quietly into the background of her mind. She hung up her cape, donned her apron, and did her daily round of chores. There was still the visit to her father to get through, but that would not be today.

She wondered how her brother was doing at the inn. He'd married the widow who owned it, and had been very busy learning the business in the past year. His correspondence had been warm and open, but she sensed he'd felt in over his head at first. When she went to see her father, she would stop in at the inn, since they both lived on the eastern edge of Glasgow.

Once her small repast was finished, Orla sighed in satisfaction and finally opened the letter.

"Very well," she said. "Let's have it out."

As she read, she tried to remember the particulars of the reading of the will that day, months ago, when she'd felt muzzy-headed and dim with all the new information.

The solicitor, Mr. Gittlings, begged leave to call her attention to a new opportunity in investments that would be a superb fit for her capital.

Was it a bad fit currently, she wondered. Why the prompt attention, when she had never known the solicitor to initiate business with her husband in their decade of transactions?

Mr. Gittlings went on to introduce the new fund being offered at a handsome nine per cent return; it was to do with railway ventures, the latest invention to bring British commerce more immediately to British citizens.

I know what a railway venture is, Mr. Gittlings, Orla thought, piqued. She threw down the letter, exasperated at the way this kicked up the dust of all the adjustments she'd already made peace with. The nest egg was the thing to be counted on and never touched. That was how Robert had set it up, and she trusted him. Who was this solicitor, to think he knew her own welfare better?

The pleasant mood from Isobel's conversation was spoiled. Orla sighed.

"Bring British commerce more immediately to British citizens. That sounds..."

It sounded fine until Orla thought of all the places round the globe that Britain lay claim to, where British citizens lived. That would be...a lot of railways. She hadn't seen one yet, only heard the secondhand description of how they worked at a dinner with the new minister. No, this was not something she wanted to get mixed up in. It seemed altogether too fast for her new, quiet, respectable life. She wanted to pursue her own interests, advance the little education she'd improved on during her marriage. She aspired to learn the pianoforte.

Well, that was going to take a little maneuvering, but what she *could* do that week was explore the lending library and take a newspaper. That had been revolving in her mind for some time and she was ready to engage in that small new step. The railways would have to wait.

The next morning Orla carefully wrote her notes to her southern friends as to dates and times of arrival and dropped these at the post office in Town. The hansom that brought her in was able to direct her to the street with the lending library, one she had never heard of but whose number was not too high.

When she found the sign on the building, it was apparent why she'd not heard of Threadneedle Street: it ran the length of one bank of buildings, starting with a respectable three-storied bulk and ending with a sagging squat affair. Of course the library she'd chosen was in this last. Orla sighed to herself and chided herself for taking library suggestions from a neighbor who didn't read.

But then she entered the space and the air was so still she felt she'd stepped into a tomb. She sniffed. The chemical smells of ink and metal type mixed with new leather bindings and musty old pages—it went right to her head, restricted as such smells had been to her for most of her life. She glanced around, wondering at the lack of a salesman or proprietor to hover over her. Then she set to roaming.

The first half of the shop contained waist-height square tables of books and rails with papers hanging over, the tiny type making her turn her head sideways. She edged her way around a few of these, squinting several times at their content. New publications presented, meetings of the magistrates, public auctions to be had—but this was all petty, daily stuff. She wanted to learn about the policies of Government.

She proceeded around the square islands until she approached the back half of the space in which there were tall shelves in ranked aisles and more than a few shady corners.

"Books," she breathed reverently.

"Yes," came the mild answer on her right. Orla's breath caught at her shock; she hadn't noticed the approach of the slight, smooth-faced man. He wore a dark suit and held a pair of spectacles in his folded hands. "May I help madam?"

Blinking briefly to stop herself from looking around for a 'madam'—surely another creature couldn't have crept up with as little noise—she inclined her head.

"I'm sorry, I didn't hear you," she said.

"I'm sorry, I didn't mean to startle you," he replied. "Your first visit?"

"Yes. I was looking for…" She hesitated, not wanting to be lectured about women and money matters. "Well, I was interested in learning about investments. How the banks do it, how the Government does it, that sort of thing?"

"Indeed. If I may enquire, this is for yourself, not a book as a gift?"

"Oh, no."

"Well, that is not a specialty of this place, but I could doubtless find some if I ask some of my colleagues. Does madam have securities she is curious about, in a general way?"

"Mmm," Orla replied, non-committal. "I am curious about the Three Per Cents, and opinions about the railway stocks and shares." His eyebrows rose and she hastened to reassure him. "They have been recommended to me but they sound rather unsafe, so I wanted to hear a different opinion about what else people invest in."

She wasn't displaying any cleverness but at least she was being circumspect.

"I see. Of course, an excellent notion. Does madam take a paper currently?"

"Oh, do please call me Mrs. Smith. I'm nothing so grand as to need a French-sounding title. But no, I don't. I was hoping to leave here with one."

"There is the *Glasgow Herald*. That would cover all the goings-on in town, if madam—if you were interested in the local news."

"What about that other *Herald* I saw—*Herald to the Trades*?"

"—*Advocate*, yes. That is an old issue; it has been shut down. It is quite a different sort of paper, ma'am. Rather more like the *Scottish Trades' Union Gazette* you see here; that's still being printed."

"Ah. Does this *Gazette* talk about how to invest the country's money responsibly?"

"It does."

"It seemed to cover more interesting news than the first one, when I was glancing through."

"Indeed."

She asked the price, which seemed reasonable given her weekly income, and she wrote her name on the ledger for subscribers, feeling rather pleased with herself.

"Are you the proprietor here?"

"Yes, ma—yes, Mrs. Smith."

They continued with a few pleasantries about new acquaintances before she realized she was about to leave without learning his name.

"And to whom may I direct my requests about investment books?"

"Apologies," said the man. "My name is McNary, ma'am. And I'll be happy to answer future requests."

Chapter 3

By the next week, Orla had received confirmations for her travel plans and received her first edition of the *Scottish Trades' Union Gazette*. She compared it to the stories being reported in the national paper available at the butcher's and was quite astonished that the woes of the cotton spinners had not gotten a single inch in the latter.

Other stories included were about corresponding society aims, the Corn Laws—that one was in every paper—and various trials taking place that she didn't know or care about. She took note of stories about the cotton spinners in the next week's paper as well, for her father had been one when she was growing up, and she'd been familiar with the factory rhythms for a good eight years before she was employed by the rector. She hadn't a clue they were as destitute as all this, but then she lived outside town, and away from the factories now. She cut out the columns and pasted them to a square of stiff card and considered it a new project: a guard book of her education.

After that session with the *Gazette*, she was ready to set out for her usual summer visits, feeling quite well set up with her three new gowns. She'd engaged the hansom to transport her and her trunk and valise to the coaching inn early that May morning and was surprised to find a solid and well-dressed man stepping out of the carriage as she walked up to it.

"Pardon me, ma'am," he said, touching his hat as he held the door open and offered her his hand. As he swept her up the steps, she was surprised by a strong scent of caramel. It so overwhelmed her senses that she could barely remember where she was heading, or why, as she sat on the lumpy cushion, unable to look away from the man. Almost too late, she blurted out a thank you. His prominent brow, raised with expectation, dropped. He bowed slightly and headed off. The smoky sweetness from his presence in the carriage lingered. It was the closest interaction with a male stranger she'd had since her mourning. She clutched her valise and waited for the driver.

When he came, she asked if he knew the name of his last passenger. It was horribly indiscreet but the question was out before she could stop herself; at least she asked it with an even voice.

The driver barely glanced at her as he secured her trunk to the back of the carriage. Apparently she was sized up and dismissed from the running of the marriage stakes that fast. *Better that way,* she told herself.

"Oh, that was a Mister Tate, missus. New to the neighborhood, but seen him a few times lately. Interested in snapping up some of the old duke's property or the like, should be my guess."

"Thank you," she said in as unconcerned a voice as she could muster. So this was the subject of Isobel's carefully dropped gossip: Mr. Tate the Younger, heir to the sugar warehouses in Port Glasgow and the lucrative trade contracts with Dominica and St. Vincent. He hadn't had the assuming air that she had expected someone of such affairs to carry with them, but perhaps he was an affable sort. She chided herself. Orla Rose Rafferty Smith was the very ragged ruffle at the bottom of the neighborhood's social set dressing, and yet she could imagine the sighs of the young Shaw ladies meeting such a man. When she pictured this, she could laugh at herself a little, and was relieved.

Off she went on her journey, and worried no more about what the gossip mill would do with Mr. Tate in her absence.

The first leg of the journey was uneventful; May was not as popular a time as Easter for traveling and Orla shared the carriage with only one other couple. When they had changed horses and started out again, the couple left and was replaced by a gentleman who, though well-dressed, smelled of salted fish. Orla snuggled deeper into her cloak and shawl and prayed the second leg was shorter than she recalled.

It was not. The smell dissipated after an hour but Orla was sure it meant only that now she, too, would smell like salted fish. *Ah, well. Mrs. Darcy will forgive a great deal of her travelers,* Orla thought, smiling.

She was dropped at a lonely crossroads in high moor country but needn't have worried. Her friend's coachman was waiting in the mist for the stage to pass by.

"Oh, it is very good to see you there, John. I do hope you have not been waiting long."

She said it for formality's sake, since of course he had. He replied in the same vein.

"No, ma'am. Welcome to Northumberland. Mrs. Darcy wanted me to inform you that dinner would be at the regular hour, so you can order up a plate to your room and recover from your journey in peace, the night."

"How thoughtful. I'm glad they didn't wait dinner for me. We'll be much later than they are used to dining, won't we?"

"Aye, ma'am."

The coachman removed the blankets from the horses and secured her small trunk. It was less than an hour to the Darcys' stately home, and though it was dark as they rolled through their land, Orla recollected in her mind practically every vista on the way, as this was perhaps her dozenth visit to her friends here. While she and Robert had moved house several times at the church's whims, her time here in Northumberland had sparked her closest friendship. She sighed with pleasure, anticipating the renewal of that friendship.

That night was restful as Mrs. Darcy intended it to be, but the next morning Orla was woken abruptly by the pounding of feet in the hallway outside her door.

"Aunt Smith! Aunt Smith! It is well past breakfast, they will be putting away the dishes, nearly—you had better—"

Orla hurried to wrap her dressing gown around her and open the door. An urchin of six years stood a respectful distance away, grinning at her with missing teeth. Scrubbing at her tired eyes, Orla cleared her throat before drawing herself up to survey the little lord.

"Master Oliphaunt, I presume," she said soberly.

"You remembered! She remembered!" His eyes lit up as he ran to the top of the stairs and called down to some of his siblings. Orla was glad little Colin remembered her from two years ago. They'd played several memorable games of charades together and beat other family members, most notably by knowing the sign for an elephant.

"Colin," she said his name quietly. "I will be down to breakfast directly. Is everyone else in the parlor, or—"

"Mother and Father are in the parlor, but my sisters are still at breakfast. But it's almost over," he warned.

"Then you had better go off and let me make myself presentable!"

The little boy turned around immediately and pelted down the stairs, making for the breakfast room, where, if experience was her teacher, Orla expected he would be firing questions at his older sisters while they tried to eat. She washed quickly and put on another half-mourning gown, a lighter violet that had reminded her of iced sugar plums. The chambermaid had not yet had a chance to unpack her dresses for the week so there was still a large crease from its being in the trunk. Orla shook it out and shrugged; the weight would flatten the fold soon enough over her petticoats. Traveling did create so much extra fuss. If it wasn't for such good friends living so far away, she would never bother.

When she entered the breakfast room, two very prim young ladies were sitting side by side, one in yellow, one in blue. They were well turned out in their light day dresses, and didn't give her creases a second look.

"Aunt Smith! You're here—"

"Aunt Smith, we couldn't wait to see you—"

"—we missed you last year, and—"

"—Mama was ever so pleased—"

To this leapfrogging was added a clearing of a throat. Orla turned back toward the door through which she had come.

"Oh, Lizzie, I'm so happy to see you!"

"Dearest Orla, we are so glad you've come!"

They embraced with little pecks on the cheek and heartfelt squeezing of hands. Lizzie encouraged her to sit down while she went about making her a plate of the eggs, toast, tomatoes, and bacon, the bits which she knew Orla preferred, all the while inviting commentary on her journey and her news.

It was a feminine breaking of the fast; she could see the husband had been tasked with keeping Colin occupied elsewhere so that she could take her meal in peace. Once Lizzie saw that she was relaxed and satiated, she suggested they withdraw to the parlor to join 'the men.' The girls smiled at this. Orla felt so content to be in this sweet family circle that the pang of not having her own only struck a distant echo.

Chapter 4

Conversation in the parlor revolved around plans for the coming week's diversions, including teaching Orla to drive the horse in a gig, since the girls were also learning, visits from some of the neighbors, and even a portraitist coming to do a study of Mrs. Darcy.

"How remarkable," said Orla. "Who is the painter? How did he come to be acquainted with the family?"

"One of last year's exhibitors in London," Mrs. Darcy supplied. "Jonathan bought one of his paintings and broached the subject. Apparently there has been quite the flurry of correspondence over it; I can't imagine why." She gave her husband a sly smile, and Orla missed what she alluded to, but it was quickly passed over.

"And doesn't it take a long time for an artist to do the painting? I remember reading it was quite tiresome for the subject."

"Perhaps with some artists, but this one has assured us he only requires three one-hour sittings. Standards, he calls his rules." Mr. Darcy's tone was dismissive.

Orla cast a look at the twins. "And is it only Mrs. Darcy he is to…"

"Quite. The twins are not old enough to grasp the honor."

"But their coming out will be soon, Jonathan. Only two years."

"True enough. Don't hurry it along, I beg you."

Another rueful, understanding smile passed between them.

"Might I have the chance to hear some playing in the evenings? I do love hearing your pianoforte, Lizzie."

"Oh, yes, of course! I will give you some sample of my latest pieces, and the twins can offer you their show pieces in turn." Mrs. Darcy lifted an eyebrow in their direction. Lily, in yellow, hunched down the slightest bit, until her sister Marianne buttressed her with a shoulder. Orla observed all the family goings-on with fascination, reading within each gesture a history.

When they had tired of discussing the week's amusements, talk turned toward Orla's new station, with an owned cottage and a secure annuity. Lizzie asked her about any changes she was keen on making, now that she'd had time to consider.

"Oh, a few," she answered. "But nothing big. I am happy with my circle of acquaintances, you know. I did think of taking lessons on the pianoforte..."

"Did you! Oh, that's wonderful, Orla. I know how you appreciate music so." Lizzie beamed at her, and Orla felt a thrill of confidence up her spine.

"Yes, now the hope is that I can get these fingers to appreciate it too!"

The day was very fine for Northumberland and the family entertained Orla out of doors for the afternoon. She was happy to see all her clothes aired and pressed when she returned to dress for dinner, and even though it was *en famille*, she really tried to practice being witty and engaging. She knew guests were coming, and she knew her social skills had rusted a bit. Thankfully, the twins and Mr. Darcy helped her reorient herself on the current topics.

Sunday morning they went to church together, the family occupying the first pew. The sermon was about the evils of being a debtor or a creditor: Orla suspected the minister of being the victim of a bad speculation from the disapproving set of his lips when he spoke of borrowing money to make money. 'Confidence tricksterism,' he called it. She knew Lizzie would be thinking, just as she was, of the high-flying kings of the finance ministry protesting being lumped in with the gypsies at the fair with their crystal balls. True, both could be accused of trying to make money from nothing, but one tended to expect more compunction from the first kind.

After church, their walk was cut short by very stormy skies, after which Orla got her wish of hearing the piano played, and learning a bit of the keyboard notes herself. After dinner, she was feeling drowsily content when she thought to ask her friend a question. They sat in Lizzie's boudoir, a dressing room-turned-study where she had her writing desk.

"Lizzie."

"Mmm?"

"You know I told you the reason for the visit to London—the change in investment prompted by the solicitor? What do you think of it?"

Mrs. Darcy readjusted herself from where she'd been reclining and set her hands on her knees to lean forward.

"I would think the man would know his business, still it is good to be circumspect. Was he ever in trouble while your husband was alive?"

"No...but I don't believe Robert would have felt easy enough with our savings to go into any schemes, even if Mr. Gittlings had offered them. I just feel that letter had a 'sidling up' quality."

"Ah. Insincere."

"Yes. It would not do to be taken advantage of."

"No, of course not, Orla."

"So how much do you familiarize yourself with your husband's investments?"

It wasn't an unexpected question to follow, but Mrs. Darcy appeared gobsmacked.

"Do you know, I've never concerned myself with Jonathan's three per cents and bonds and such. They change so little, there's never been a discussion."

Orla relaxed a little at that evidence. "You see? I shouldn't be bothered to move my portion, then."

A small silence followed. Orla looked at her friend, whose brow was furrowed, an unusual occurrence in her merry social whirl.

"Ordinarily, I would counsel a friend to ask questions about everything there is to know, of course," she said quietly. "But thinking of your case, I realize that anything might happen, and I—" She stopped herself short and looked up at Orla with a pleading expression. "I didn't mean—"

"I'm fine, Lizzie."

"But I don't know that I would be," she said firmly. "All the more reason to be aware of my assets before anything happens. There, you've inspired me to a new pursuit. We shall broach the subject with Mr. Darcy when we are next in the parlor of an evening, and see what he can tell us both."

"Excellent. I look forward to it."

Orla thought about the pleading look, an apology for alluding to Robert's sudden illness and death. She, being less attached to her husband, had lost him. Lizzie, being the more attached, still had hers. It was nobody's fault, only Fate's. But they could all take a lesson from it to be prepared to fend for themselves.

Chapter 5

When the next evening's conversational opportunity presented itself, Mrs. Darcy introduced the topic of financial knowledge and received a frown from her husband.

"Are you worried about such things?" he asked her. Their dinner guest Sir Humphreys was the justice of the peace one county over, attending the assizes.

"Well, not at the moment, but in talking with Mrs. Smith, my eyes have been opened as to the prudence of being at least familiar with them. She journeys to London to speak with her solicitor about a possible change in her investments."

"Oh, yes?" He sounded curious, not overly concerned, as he set out the pieces for a chess game.

"Yes, and I wondered if you might have advice for her," finished his wife.

"I would very much appreciate your views on the proper amount of risk to take, and which bank or agent might be the most trustworthy, Mr. Darcy. Or Sir Humphreys, if you have views on the subject as well."

Orla smiled, hoping that Mr. Darcy felt flattered but not too much. He still sometimes exhibited the sudden umbrage he had once shown when he first met them both, in Hampshire.

"Well, of course, I am glad to be of any assistance, but without the specifics, I'm not sure I'd be of much help." His fingers still plucked at knights and rooks, situating them just so on the board.

"Mr. Gittlings wants me to transfer my portion into railway shares."

That brought his head up.

"Goodness." She heard the shock in his reaction. "That would not have been my recommendation for a woman alone," he said more quietly.

"Certainly not," echoed Sir Humphreys, though Orla read not shock in his tone but disapproval of women having investments in the first place.

"What would you recommend, then?" she asked, matching his gravity.

"Well, the three per cents would be my first inclination, but I haven't given the matter close attention. Our capital is principally held in the land itself, and it is in buying and selling from year to year that the cash revenues are allocated for various costs. Very little stays in cash to go to a bank, you see. Only when there is a large outside project or cost."

"Of course. You do not count yourself as a shareholder in any of the joint stock companies then?"

His eyes flared up at her from his chess board again. "No... well, there is potential for a railway company using land by the river road, but it does not cut into much of the field and when we discussed it, we thought it would be more sensible to be part of the venture ourselves than to merely acquiesce to another board of...well. Beside that one possibility, no joint-stock shares."

Orla noticed Lizzie was listening very carefully to her husband. Probably this was news to her.

"You discussed it with the nearby land owners?" she hazarded a guess.

"Yes." Mr. Darcy indicated Sir Humphreys, who nodded.

So that was the 'we' he meant. "So if I'm understanding your reasoning, it is sensible for the landholder to have stock in a company that affects his land's value, but it is unnecessarily risky for a woman without that incentive to hold stock in a large venture with similar aims, or expansion plans. That is correct?"

"More or less, yes."

"That is helpful, Mr. Darcy. Thank you for explaining."

They passed to a round of chess, first the men facing off, then the ladies, then the winners. It ended up being husband and wife, and Orla was happy to be able to congratulate her friend at the end of the night. She retired, feeling quite spent, but lay puzzling through the various reactions she had observed for an hour in bed. Darcy had not been much help after all.

Her trip plans were to go to London at the beginning of next week, then on to Hampshire to stay with the Burches for a fortnight before returning home. Perhaps her friend Deborah or her husband would have more specific experience with investing. So resolving, she finally let sleep claim her.

The visit with the Darcys went extremely well, as expected, and she felt buoyed on the stage-coach to London the next week. She installed herself in the coaching inn and had a leisurely couple hours before her appointment with Mr. Gittlings. She refreshed herself after the journey and had a small dinner before setting out to meet him.

The waiting room at her solicitor's held two other people, reminding her that he shared his offices with other solicitors for economy. One was dressed well but not ostentatiously, his sober mien emanating gravity and some sorrow. Perhaps in the same situation as she a year ago, mourning someone. And the other was a heavily veiled woman with a baby. Orla wondered at her being here unescorted, but then perhaps the servants and carriage waited outside.

In this weather? Heartless, she thought. It wasn't exactly precipitating, but the grime of London was certainly being whipped about by unwholesome breezes, and the cold did penetrate if one wasn't well wrapped.

Each guest was called in turn. The sober-looking man emerged from his interview looking more tired, his face lined, but relieved. She wished him well. The heavily veiled woman— well, it was hard to gauge her feelings when Orla couldn't see her face, but—her shoulders seemed to have lost whatever starch had kept them squared and strong. She'd wilted. *Perhaps there is no carriage and servants waiting*, Orla thought, a bit humbled.

When at last it was her turn, no one else waited in the room. It was almost five o'clock, so she wasn't surprised. She would have to find another hansom to take her back to the inn, an annoyance which she tucked away in her mind as she sat across from Mr. Gittlings.

"Mrs. Smith, so good of you to come in person," he drawled. Orla was not a fan of the fashionable London drawl. In fact, it vexed her, bringing up old memories of snubs and gossip. He meant to imply she had no business making a complete trip out of such a minor errand, that she read well enough.

"Thank you for seeing me, Mr. Gittlings. I did so want to sort out any confusion so that I am not wrong-footed in any way. You mentioned in your letter moving my capital to some stocks that had a higher rate of return, but I wanted to inquire more particularly about them, and about the stock that I have currently. What is the difference? Why did Mr. Smith choose the lower one before?"

"Ah, I see, yes." The lanky gentleman with his flagging collar drew himself up to respond. "Your late husband did make a very fair choice in the government's three per cent bond. That was the best on offer at the time. However, in recent years, other opportunities have come to light and I thought it best to advise you of those—"

Before he could continue in that voice reserved for slow children, Orla interrupted. "Is it in any way related to the slavery bonds?"

"Is what related, ma'am?"

"Either my annuity or the new opportunities you're suggesting I pursue."

"Your annuity in the consols, ma'am."

"How so?"

And then she listened with a glad heart to the voice reserved for slow children as he explained about government bonds and debt and the twenty million pounds the government had recently promised to former slave-owners.

"So my capital is repaying the Government, who is repaying the slave-owners?"

"Former slave-owners, but yes, ma'am."

"I see..."

But Orla hesitated. She wished Lizzie or her husband had had more information. But it was entirely reasonable not to be hasty, and perhaps seek out another opinion. "Do you know, Mr. Gittlings, I think I will need to consider this more, and perhaps not at the end of a long travel day. Could I make an appointment with you after my visit to Hampshire, in a fortnight?"

They set the hour for the appointment and she made a tidy escape. The pavement outside the solicitor's office was dark and bustling, and she was a long time hailing a hansom to take her back to her inn, where she had a tolerably good supper laid. If Deborah and her husband had no particular knowledge of bonds either, what should she do? She knew no other professionals or gentlemen who would be of use, unless she were to presume on her new acquaintance with the bookseller, who seemed helpful. She sighed. Gittlings was a weasel of a solicitor, like any other. She had no doubt his fee went up if her interest did so. She would have to educate herself somehow, and learn what was the right decision.

In another day she had finished the few errands she had in London and set off for the Burches' home in Hampshire. The land they owned was not as extensive as the Darcys' holdings, but their newer money had certainly conjured a beautiful home in the neoclassical style. It had gone up while Deborah had charge of her two young children, and the chaos and trouble had driven her to the quiet parsonage many a time to chat with Orla, while her husband harangued the masons and carpenters.

Now the children were older, away at school much of the year, and Deborah had consequently developed new interests to indulge in their absence. No sooner had Orla alighted from the carriage than the familiar onslaught began, for Deborah was a woman brimming over with enthusiasm, though it wasn't always evident from the sly, cool looks she gave in company. Orla had felt the condescension or pity of the woman's inviting her to stay, but the years had pressed any awkwardness from their encounters. Now she enjoyed the open enthusiasm, in small doses.

Apparently what she had missed in the past two years was a fondness for small dogs that would follow her around and fight over the space on the sofa.

"Dearest Mrs. Smith!" Mrs. Burch was calling down the drive as she strode forward, which is when Orla saw at least five small dogs with curly tails and black faces trailing her. She claimed Orla's arm and left no room to negotiate. "You are the event of the day, my dear, otherwise we would perish from boredom. How was your journey? Oh, you've made a friend in Barnabas, look at that. Come now, tell me all about your stop in London, or at least the most interesting parts. Whom did you see—"

The continuous stream of talk did not cease until they were seated in the parlor and Mrs. Burch despatched a servant for the tea. Then, with all the dogs but no people in the room, the lady took a deep breath and beamed at her visitor. "You look very well, Orla. How are you feeling?"

And Orla was able to answer at her own speed. She heard about the pugs, and she told about the news that passed for excitement in her home parish of Crookston.

"Perish of boredom, indeed," drawled Deborah. "But we have a rigorous program for you starting tomorrow, darling. We invited simply everyone in the neighborhood to come admire you, or buoy you up if that was needed. Thank you," she said when the footman came in to lay the tea.

"I don't believe I need buoying up at present, but I do appreciate you going to all the trouble, Deborah." Orla smiled. "You know I'd rather be an observing statue than a guest of honor, though I know that is not what you have planned."

She explained about her wish to learn the pianoforte, at which this friend also exclaimed at the ease of such an endeavor. Orla felt a brief pang under her breastbone at hearing it again. *When you grow up expecting to learn to play, of course it is easy,* she thought. *But when you never thought you would, and you're past the age where accomplishments are necessary, is it possible to learn purely from occasional devotion?* She wasn't sure, but she'd plucked up the courage to try. Then she came around to the initial reason for her sojourn in London.

"Mr. Gittlings doesn't strike me as overly trustworthy," she hemmed. "But that could simply be my lack of experience with solicitors. I would greatly appreciate your and Mr. Burch's opinions on investing."

"Oh, Declan? He'll have a whole lecture prepared on the subject, so do not ask until you are sitting with your paper and pen." Deborah joked but Orla knew she and Declan got along well, though they weren't as besotted with each other as Lizzie and Jonathan.

"Well, there should be room for a short lecture in the next ten days, should there not? What with the many guests at the house being able to entertain each other."

"If you can follow him, so much the better, my dear. It's all over my head." Deborah laughed a low, throaty laugh. Orla felt the difference of her own need to know to fight for her interests compared to that of her friends, still wives, remaining blissfully ignorant, though Lizzie hoped they would change that.

Deborah must have seen a shadow of that bereft feeling cross her face, for she asked if she was well.

"Oh, yes. Just thinking of the vast possibilities sometimes fatigues, you know." She smiled wanly and her friend took a sip of her tea, 'hmm'-ing in agreement. She reached over to pat Orla's knee.

"We shall have all the guests or none of the guests, just as you prefer, Orla. It's so good to see you again." Orla shook her head faintly at her friend's whimsical generosity and chuckled.

"Well, let's see the list."

Chapter 6

The list turned out to contain a countess, a baron, a very successful tradesman, a very accomplished poet-critic, and a pair of Quakers from America, relatives of Mr. Burch. Orla had interesting conversations with each of them, and received several lessons on the pianoforte from the countess.

"Just wait," said Lady Burgess. "It's all a delight now, but then your fingers won't move fast or far enough and you'll find yourself feeling wretchedly unsuited. But that will pass, too, eventually. It happens to the best more often than they like to admit," she added. "Just enjoy pursuing what you love to hear, is my advice."

The tradesman, a Mr. Mackenzie, had strong opinions when she asked about investments and the government bonds just issued.

"Speculation is life-blood, no doubt about it. 'S what keeps the Empire going, all that money circulating, all that hope gambling on who will succeed. Makes my own blood thrill to even speak of it." His smile was a grimace, but Orla tried to engage him.

"So you would recommend it even for a widow's portion? But how is she to discern—"

"Well, now, that's all about who she has for advisors, and where they are placed to hear of solid bets." He put a finger to the side of his rather red nose. "Sometimes those in Government can help, and sometimes they're the last to know."

"Then whom might you suggest I—"

"My good woman, the only thing to be putting money in nowadays is the railways. If you're not keen on sniffing out a bargain, it's got to be the railways."

Orla gave up. He would not let her finish a sentence. Still, it was another vote for the railways. The Quakers had a very different view when they came to dine, tending more toward Darcy's protectiveness of the land.

"I won't say I saw sparks," Deborah said as she sat with Orla on their last morning together. "But I might have seen steam coming out of Mr. Mackenzie's ears."

Orla smiled. "I admire their sticking to their principles. And having a tight-knit community such as they seem to have is no doubt a boon for information, just like knowing a Government official might be."

"You think so? Mmm." Deborah mused for a moment, then sighed. "I wish I could hear of you in a tight-knit community up north, or at least an amusing set of characters, but it doesn't sound as if there is very much to keep you there, except that cottage," she added, inclining her head.

"Yes, I suppose I could sell it and find somewhere else, but they say it is not a good time to sell."

"Certainly not. You've got many good years left. There must be another boom of prosperity coming that will give you some interesting choices. If not in neighbors, then in neighborhoods," she teased.

After a few more friendly words, Orla heard the clock in the hall and stood to take leave of her hostess. "It was most stimulating, and educational, and of course a joy to see you well and hear the family are well."

"You are always an education in yourself, Mrs. Smith, so do come round again whenever you are in reach, if your business should take you down here again before next year."

Orla walked down to the waiting carriage that would take her to London, where she would meet with her solicitor again. She left her trunk at her favorite inn and proceeded to Gittlings' office at the appointed time, not seeing anyone in the anteroom this time.

A clerk came to greet her and ushered her into his office immediately. After a few polite words, Orla laid out her intention.

"Not to move any of your capital?" Gittlings repeated, incredulous. "But who has convinced you of such a decision? It's practically criminal..."

"Be that as it may, but I do not feel easy about altering the choice Robert made at this time. I am educating myself on the choices and may in time decide otherwise, but I am not yet persuaded it would be right for my—my outlook."

He looked less incredulous after this speech, but still doubtful.

"I am taking a newspaper. I am reading up on the state of things. I have had good advice from those of my friends well placed to know about it." She spoke a bit defensively and lowered her chin so she wouldn't feel like a schoolgirl standing up to a teacher.

"Well," he spoke brusquely. "This is not what I expected. I can certainly continue as you wish. I'm only sorry you've had the whole of a journey to London to do nothing."

She ignored the acerbic comment. "I had other matters to see to, but I appreciate your concern," she said. Her business concluded, she departed, feeling if not seeing the furor she left behind her. *Oh, when man does not get his way,* she thought. *En garde.*

Instead of worrying about what some solicitor might think of her pea-brained financial intelligence, she took herself back to her inn and wrote the letter to her father that would set the date for her arrival and proposed visit. She also wrote to her brother that she would need a room that week, and could pay. A delicate matter, both the pride of her brother and the reception from her father. Still, it was done.

The next morning, she was on the stage-coach with her trunk and valise before dawn, to face five grueling days on the road.

Chapter 7

The last coach pulled into the yard of her brother's inn in good time for tea, for which Orla was quite ready. While the air in the yard was not as fresh as she might like, it was a step above the closeness of the air in the tavern on the ground floor. Pipe smoke and dark wood made the place feel older than it was, built only fifty years ago or so. She told the bar-maid in the kitchen window her business and heard her shouting for Master Rafferty a moment later.

Her brother scurried down narrow steps and his alert eyes found her immediately. He darted a glance to the kitchen, seemed to ascertain that everything was fine, then walked up to embrace Orla.

"My dear sister, thank you for the note. I was pleased to get it, and the notice that we'd be seeing you. Welcome, and have you only just arrived? Ah, well, let's get you settled."

Her brother was jovial, affable, a little rumpled in any situation, but possessed of good common sense. They had grown up closer than their other siblings, who were several years younger. But her marriage and conversion had offended her father, and the siblings played a game of hide and seek to visit her only when they wouldn't face their father's wrath in doing so. Now that she was a widow, she wondered what he would do. At least her brother always had a moment for her.

He settled her into one of the snugs in the private bar and went to fetch some provender. Orla lay her valise on the seat beside her and leaned back on the wood for a moment, feeling the lumpy bumpy rolling of the carriage against her backside finally fade away.

"Fish pie and mushroom soup, cure for what ails you," he said as he slid the plate and bowl in front of her. "Speak of ale, be right back with it," he said.

"Or a sherry," she said, at half-loud volume, since she couldn't decide whether it would be embarrassing to voice her preference. He came back with a cream sherry and cutlery, waggling his eyebrows.

"Sherry tippler, eh? My, my, you have turned your back— only kidding, Orla, don't let me knock you off your block. You've done fine and well enough, I say." He made his face serious, lowering his brow and pursing his lips, thin though they were.

"My condolences, Orla. Truly. How are you feeling?"

She already had the spoon in hand for the fish pie, which was making her mouth water, but felt awkward with the introduction of a new topic. She set the spoon down deliberately.

"Thank you, Christopher. I do appreciate it. It was a happy marriage, no matter that we were not—blessed—with children. I—don't especially miss having a man around the house, but I do miss him making some of the decisions." She picked up her spoon and broke into the pie to let some steam escape.

"Well, that's all right. What a man's for, I'd wager. What are you deciding on at the minute?"

Orla shouldn't have been surprised, but her brother posing the question like that took her off guard.

"Oh, erm, you know. Social engagements and meals and bills, investments, things like that." He nodded and seemed content with her answer. "But Christopher, how are you and your wife doing? And how is Father?" she finished in an undertone.

"Oh, we manage." The simple words concealed a lot, she knew. "Serena is a general at arms if ever I saw one—which I haven't, of course—but she makes this place run. Speak of decisions! I'm kept busy running to do even half the things she looks after. But we're happy. I like her children, though children they won't be for much longer!"

Orla listened to him patter on about the goings-on of the busy family. His eyes were alight, first with merriment then with emotion. This was a more open side to her brother than she'd seen. Did that bode well for the meeting with their father?

"And Father?" She repeated when he had a lull in his tidings so that he looked around to assure himself everyone was satisfied in the dining area.

"Oh, him. We see him at Mass about once a month. Brings his new family. Blessed awkward, his new wife being so young and ignorant. But they're civil. My Serena is more than civil; we've had them in for supper twice this year, though they don't return the favor."

Orla worked to control her breathing through this status report. She'd known through Christopher that her father was married a decade ago, but not that there had been more children. *Has it really been that long?* She supposed it had. *And they went to Mass, as Christopher's children did. Of course, the men didn't need to convert to Episcopalian to fit in.* She tamped down on the old resentment and focused on her brother's words.

"We're happy to put you up in the room above the private bar." He pointed at the ceiling. "Not much used unless there's a big do. Should be nice and quiet for you. And then you'll see Father in the morn?"

"Aye—yes. I've sent ahead. I'll leave my trunk here until I return for the hansom home."

"Sounds sensible." Her brother smiled as his eyes went to her plate. "Good, isn't it?"

She glanced down at the fish pie. It was rich and savory, and somehow she'd already made half of it disappear. "Delicious!"

"That's my Serena's own receipt. I can give it to you if you like, she has me get the ingredients every week, know them off by heart."

"I should like that, Christopher. I'll poke my head into the kitchen on my way up to thank her."

She'd eaten early and heavily; she needed time to digest before falling asleep, though her bones ached from the journey still. The room she was in was homely, with a cheery fire. Even though it was the start of summer, the nights cooled quick round here, and the summer storms could douse a person in a blink. There was a high, well-stuffed bed, a wash-stand, a small cupboard, and a small table and chair.

Orla sat with her writing desk on her lap, staring far beyond the fire, sorting through her feelings. She could deal with each adjustment individually, just not together. The finances piece she would leave as it was and see what the newspapers could tell her. The piece with her father's new family—that hurt, but she had a duty to pay to him. He had raised her and Christopher as well as he could when their mother died in childbed. She wondered if he was choosing to raise his children differently now.

No matter, she reminded herself. Flustered at this train of thought, she pulled out the newspaper she'd bought in London, figuring she might as well start it now. It was an abolitionist, anti-Union paper, and she rather liked the by-line:

"Ignorance the base of all Despotism and Misery.

Knowledge the root of Liberty and Happiness."

Now it distracted her to read about all the various happenings in Parliament, in London, in the halls of Westminster.

She was absorbed in a tale of a lawsuit involving slander of a Peer when she was disturbed by a large shout. It was followed by low rumbling of what might be laughter, but it seemed to be so close! She put down the paper and peered into all corners of the small room, testing out where she could hear it the clearest.

The sounds had moved from laughter to speech, and she found if she stood looking into the cupboard with its doors open, she could catch the conversation fairly clearly from the private bar below. She was listening to a bunch of old men toss back ribald jokes. Shocking!

They lapsed into lower voices and long silence and she lost interest, turning to sit back down to her newspaper. But then a sharp word spoken caught her ear: *Indian muslin.*

She turned the page back on her paper and scanned the columns for the article that still rang in her mind.

"Dhaka muslins from India increase price yet again," she read.

There now! Who were these men discussing this very scarce and highly desirable muslin? She walked back to the cupboard, paper in hand, to listen. After several minutes of various ports of trade being discussed, the men appeared to be in agreement about the impossibility of finding any true Dhaka muslin dealers.

Orla looked again at the article in her hand. *New producers of cotton challenge the Southern American States' stranglehold. India set to become new cotton king. Textile mills hedge bets; Samples of foreign cotton excite buyers.*

'Foreign'? What was foreign cotton, if not American? America had not been part of Britain since Orla had been alive, so she tsked at this old-time view. Cotton. Muslin. She didn't know much of anything about where they came from, only that her father had worked retting, cutting, and bleaching linen and later, cotton. Were these men to be trusted? She wasn't sure.

Still, it was an interesting thread, she thought, a smile creeping up her face as she realized her choice of words. *Might come in handy later.* She made a note of the ports they had named and resolved to ask her brother who had reserved the private bar. Perhaps now she had a clue about where to put her money.

Chapter 8

The hour had come; Orla raised her hand and rapped at the door with her knuckles. Though it was muted because of her leather gloves, it was soon opened by a young girl. She looked up at Orla through long lashes, not quite trusting. Which made sense, in this neighborhood.

"Good morning. I'm Mrs. Smith, here to call upon Mr. Rafferty. Is he in?"

The girl's brow furrowed. Doubt. Confusion. "O'course he's in." She backed up and waited for her to enter and closed the door with a thump. It didn't scare Orla, but it did disconcert her. This must be one of her half-sisters.

"And what's your name?"

"Not supposed to tell it to strangers," she muttered, before dashing through a short hallway to the back room. Orla hesitated then followed. The kitchen was in back, and standing in front of the hearth fire where two pots dangled from hooks was a round-faced woman with dark brown hair, swept under a kerchief. She shrieked when she caught sight of Orla.

"Olive! What you be doin' lettin' strangers intae the house, what I tell ye!"

When no answer was promptly given, the woman sighed and turned back, blinking once she realized Orla was still there, requiring dealing with.

"Ye'd be the heathen daughter, then," she accused.

"Episcopalian is not heathen, Mrs.—"

"Would ye prefer *traitorous* daughter? I t'ought not. Aye, he tol' me well enough, he's in the girls' room, mending the shoes." She jerked her chin upward, indicating there were stairs somewhere for her to find the upper story. Orla turned around and spied them to her right. She held onto her temper with both hands. If this woman got her ideas of Orla from her father, she didn't hold much hope of his having softened.

"Thank you, Mrs. Rafferty," she said. "Pleased to meet you."

She turned away to go up the stairs but felt the contempt even in the woman's nonverbal reply. She was perhaps five years younger than Orla. *Younger than I am. I wonder what desperation drove her to join forces with Father.* She had a sudden fierce dread of how her father would look after all these years.

The stairway was steep, without a banister, and she saw the floor at eye-level before gradually taking it all in: one large bed lofted up from the floor on three rows of wood and brick, one large trunk in the corner, and half a wall of hooks holding various clothing. Her father sat on a small movable stool beside the bed, with a last holding some leather against his knee. He stopped his work and looked up long enough to acknowledge her with a swallowing in his throat. Scant white locks curled around his tanned scalp. His blue eyes still pierced, though his face sagged more than the last time she'd seen it. A salt-and pepper beard was just forming, as if he'd forgotten to shave the past few days.

"Good morning, Father."

His mouth worked a moment before he mastered himself. "Orla."

She remained standing. "How are you?"

His index finger and thumb slid back and forth over the wooden form.

"We're well. And yourself?"

"I'm well."

There was a pause as each gathered the courage to say something next.

"Christopher said you'd been all the way to London. That true? What for?"

"I usually visit my friends the Darcys and the Burches in the early summer, Father. They are very good and extend an invitation. I also had some business in London. It was a satisfactory journey on all counts." *Though you didn't ask*, she thought.

"So now you're widowed. And no children, I hear?"

A spasm of pain in her abdomen made her squeeze her hand into a fist. "No children," she said as neutrally as she could.

"I'm sorry," her father said, his voice softened the tiniest measure. "Will ye come back?"

She knew he didn't mean to the new house and family, but to the True Faith.

"I'm the same person, *a athair*." Her voice rasped. How to tell him that it was all the same to her? That she remained the same solitary soul no matter where she worshipped, what she said she believed in, and how she confessed—which she did every Saturday by her bed.

His fingers were still fidgeting.

"So you're out of mourning. What will you do with yourself?" He spoke brusquely. Orla wet her lips.

"I'm trying to learn about the world now, Father." She laughed a little. "Subscribed to a newspaper and everything."

He grunted. "Which one?"

"*Scottish Trades' Union Gazette* currently. I like what they say."

He nodded acknowledgement. She tried to reach him on his own ground.

"How are the bleachfields?"

He blew out a harsh breath. "I wish they were as good as before, but there's always people improving on things, making the case for changing this and that, how things been done for a hundred years. But they'll find out. Or my replacement will, soon enough. Had forty men under me, you know."

Orla smiled. "That must've been quite a pile of humanity."

Her father tsked at her attempt at humor. "We do well enough. I just hope to God we don't get another bad year. Low orders, jobbers let go...it's no good for the people who have nothing else to do in the area."

"Can they try the thread factories?" Orla asked.

A breath hissed out through his teeth. "They might, if they wanted to be ground into the mud with an overseer stealing their time and the food from their mouths. As soon as you put yourself under someone else, by God, you're under their thumb."

Orla stayed silent, not wanting to point out that he'd just said forty men were apparently under his thumb.

"Well. Would you introduce me to your—wife? And the children? Perhaps so they don't call me a stranger next time?"

She felt like she was falling as she suggested it, so easily presuming a next time. But her father, after a slight hesitation, put down his tools and came toward the stairs. As he passed, she saw his jaw clench and wondered at the suppressed energy. Was it going well, this visit? She couldn't even be sure of that, though at least there was no yelling and screaming.

She was introduced to the two children, Marie and Ian, and their mother, Elspeth. The girl who had answered the door was in fact his grandchild, a daughter of Christopher's visiting on an errand.

Elspeth had reformed her tongue in her husband's presence but clearly, from the jut of her jaw, had not changed her prejudiced opinion. Ian ducked his head as he would have for a teacher. The boy was keen to be apprenticed to a leather tailor when he was old enough.

"But he goes to school," Elspeth said. "And he'll keep going, for the first two years of the apprenticeship. It's in the contract, til he's twelve. He'll have as good an education as any, and a trade."

She sounded defensive. Orla didn't like to comment and invite a malicious interpretation of her praise. She merely nodded and smiled.

Olive was peering at her dubiously. "Granny Elspeth says you're not to stay for dinner or tea. Do you live far away?"

She ignored the first part of her comment. "Not very far, but it would be a very long walk, indeed, so I take a carriage."

"That's dear," said Olive.

Orla bit her lip, casting around for something to say that wasn't apt to be taken as a weapon by the wife. "It is, rather, but I do like watching the horses on the street."

A minute relaxation of the girl's forehead and what might be the start of a smile rewarded her. "I do, too," she heard her say, very quietly.

They stood in the front room awkwardly until Orla concluded that was as good a first effort as there would be.

"Well, it was a pleasure to meet you all, and to see you, Father. I should be getting back to Christopher's to look after my trunk now."

The tension broke as they split up to separate tasks, mumbling replies and going to the door to see her off. Elspeth spoke no more accusing words, but gazed after her with eyes narrowed. No waving, just watching. It would be a tiresome process to ingratiate herself.

As good as could be expected, Orla reminded herself as she walked back to where the hansom cabs waited in a line. *And perhaps something to build on.*

Chapter 9

The journey was done, the meeting held, the defenses breached. Orla sat again in her kitchen on a sunny morning in late June and allowed herself to fully let go of the worry she'd been holding. She had another newspaper from Mr. McNary to peruse, but she was enjoying the morning hour in the sunlight through her open window first. Her tea half-drunk, her scone all gone, she gazed out the back of her cottage to what used to be an orchard, where a few gnarly trees still bore a slim apple crop each autumn. The path was simply trodden earth, made by the long line of denizens of this particular cottage over the generations.

She was back home in time to see the last of the flowers, gorgeous white blossoms that buzzed with delighted bees. As she was enjoying the warm haze and hum, a gray shape leapt in through the window. She shrieked and stood up so abruptly her chair toppled sideways. She recovered almost immediately. *A cat!* It now huddled under her table shaking. She let out her breath and allowed her heart to slow its wild beating and talked to the creature.

"Shh, now, it's safe in here, was someone scaring you out there now?" She glanced up out the window to see a bird circling high overhead. "Is that old hawk out there patrolling the lanes? Oh my dear, you're safe in here, it's all right." Continuing her line of susurrating sounds, the cat eventually poked its nose close enough to sniff her hand exploratively. Then as she seemed to pose no threat, it rubbed its ears along her hand; her heart melted.

"That's how it's to be, is it," she murmured. But she was happy to play godmother to a little rascal tabby for a while. She got up slowly to fetch a bowl of milk for it then took her seat at the table again and settled in to read the paper. She leaned over to squint at the small type, her whole back hunched so that when she straightened to turn the page at last, she almost yelped with the protest of sore muscles.

"Aaaoooh, this won't do at all," she muttered. "Best go ask Mr. McNary if he knows where to find a good lorgnette." And because that combination of words sounded so preposterous, she laughed out loud, scaring the cat from its lapping of the milk sufficient to stare at her suspiciously.

"Never you mind. You just stay away from the furnishings..." She narrowed her eyes at the frozen cat, wondering if she was leaving her best things open to destruction, then sighed. "Fine, you can stay, and I'll leave the window open, all right?"

She waited until its eyes eventually left her face, turning to the window whence it had come.

"I think I'll call you Levern, for the stream. Well, make yourself at home, Lev."

Feeling less drowsy and more galvanized for action, she prepared for her visit to the lending library.

On her walk to the depot, however, she heard a rap on a window pane. Miss Arbscher was summoning her into their rooms. She waved and called at their front door. *Just for a moment,* she promised herself.

"Are you well?" Miss Arbischer inquired anxiously.

"Yes, indeed, just a little fatigued after the long journey. And you, and your sister, I hope you are still in good health?"

Her hostess clucked her tongue—not an entirely polite thing to do, but Orla wouldn't censure an elder for familiarity. The older woman let forth a sigh that showed all the cares on her shoulders.

"Not that bad, I hope?" Orla asked, trying to keep her face open and serious when she wanted to roll her eyes at the woman's dramatics.

"Oh, my dear, I am glad you are well, that is all. All sorts of rumors find their way up here about the roughness of the railway for travel, you know, and while I am assured it is civilized, I would hate to hear of you having a bad turn on account of—well, the *unrest*."

The word was so clearly emphasized, Orla feared there must have been an incident. *A mob threatening violence?*

"I wasn't on a railway, Miss Arbischer, only the faithful mail coach. Did I miss something happening while I was gone? I admit to not having kept up with the national papers the last few weeks."

"Not this month, but heavens, those hotheads at the cotton mills are forever threatening, and I would not like to see you mixed up in such a stramash as Peterloo! Louise has been fretting over it, poor thing, so I took the first opportunity to make certain you were whole and all was well so I could tell her, when she returns."

"Where has she gone?" Nowhere on the railway, Orla thought, suppressing an ironic smile.

"Only over to the vicar's to contribute some posies for the dressing up of the kirk. You know, Martha's wedding is next week." The older woman's eyes shone. A mix of emotions washed over Orla. She recognized Miss Arbischer's discounting of her sister's activities as her attempt to feel equal to her even though she had never married. Her 'posies' were likely several large bouquets. And still, the thought of a young marriage got the woman teary-eyed. She hoped the envy and tenderness balanced each other out in her bosom.

"Yes, I'm certain it will be a lovely service. Well, thank you for your kind enquiries, but I must get on now. No, thank you, I couldn't. All right. That's lovely, thank you, Miss Arbischer."

She felt like a fourteen year old girl leaving like that, rather than a matron of thirty-three years, but flattery did grease the social wheels. She made it to the inn in time and was treated to a seat with no springs at all, alas. After the half hour of hard road, she felt mildly queasy but she alighted and found Threadneedle Street again. Mr. McNary was once again invisible as she entered, so she wandered slowly back to the higher shelves to peruse the book titles.

Natural philosophy, moral philosophy, mechanics of poetry —that one made her pause. Botany, history—*my, what vast stores of history the shelves hold!* From ancient Greeks, Romans, and Phoenicians to analyzing the Revolution of thirty years before. She reached for this last and heard the slightest clearing of a throat. She snatched her hand back.

"Ah, Mr. McNary. Good morning."

"Good morning, Mrs. Smith. I hope you are well after your travels?"

"Yes, thank you." She was a little surprised he remembered. Had she mentioned it? Well, obviously she had. "I had to catch up on three weeks' worth when I returned! I shan't be able to leave for any amount of time in future if I am to stay current, I see now."

McNary didn't smile but inclined his head in acknowledgment.

"And madam is interested in the Revolution now?" He inquired politely.

"Oh, it was just curiosity. I was simply impressed with the breadth of the history titles, so I wanted to rake a measure of their depth as well. But I should be asking about a stock-trading book, shouldn't I? Or an economics one."

"That depends. Did your prior study of the newspapers indicate a specific procedure or event that prompted you to learn more?"

"Mr. McNary, you are exactly right there. I did see reference to a Greek bond scandal that I did not understand. Perhaps you could direct me…?"

They talked about bonds and debt and collapse and—of course, speculation.

"There was even a MacGregor that started a scheme for emigrants to a fictional country, Mrs. Smith. Not too long ago…I believe he's in South America now."

Orla's eyes were round with incredulity. "A fictional country," she whispered. "But not the Utopia we were told of, I bet," she added with a wry smile.

"No, more like the opposite. We have had a very trying few years of schemes, there's no denying it. So many people have lost their places and had to emigrate."

Orla knew that there had been bank collapses and bad harvests but she'd only seen them through the eyes of a vicar's wife: people she needed to tend to in their hour of need.

"But then again, some few have been lucky with their guesses…or shrewd." A considering tone in his voice made Orla shift her attention to him. "Were there other mentions in the papers you had difficulty interpreting?"

"The Unstamped…?"

"Ahh, yes, that is a cause near and dear to our hearts here at the shop, for we are one of those who publish a weekly for people who cannot afford the stamp duty. The duty in effect compels us to raise funds to be able to report the news to the class of people who need to know it the most."

Orla nodded, soon knowing a great deal more of the vast array of publications up and down country that fit into this category. She quizzed him a few minutes more about the cotton spinners' articles she'd pasted in her guard book, and the cotton importing changes she'd heard rumor of. His answers set her to thinking. She thanked Mr. McNary for his time and departed with a new paper under her arm. By the time she exited the hansom at Crookston, Orla was resolved to change solicitors, and knew whom to ask.

Chapter 10

"Yes, good morning. I was passed your name by our mutual acquaintance, Mr. McNary."

Orla sat where the man indicated, on a handsome leather chair across from his desk. It was much like Gittlings' office inasmuch as it was in a busy city where she could hear the shouts from the shipyards out the window. The solicitor was nothing like the sneering London man, though.

Mr. Grant was of medium height and rather well-stuffed. He was polite without simpering or drawling. She was able to finish her sentences while he listened, which she was only now learning, when trying to do business, was a key factor in accomplishing said business.

"Of course. Mr. McNary is a good friend. We sit on a few of the same boards and committees." Before Orla could ask which boards and committees, he continued smoothly. "What help can I render you today, Mrs. Smith?"

"I want to change solicitors. And I want to change some of my stock certificates, or shares, or whatever they're called."

Again, she could never appear clever. She settled for circumspect.

"I have an annuity in the consols, but I would like to sell 5% of it and invest in one of the firms importing cotton, but not from America. I take it you are empowered to conduct such transactions?"

"Yes, I am."

"And can you do so anonymously, so that the dealers would not know they were dealing with a woman?"

The thought had occurred to her on the carriage ride into Town. She remembered Darcy saying something about not recommending the railways for a woman alone. But why? What was so raucous about a railway share that it might scandalize or influence a woman? She wanted to be treated equally, which meant, accordingly, anonymously.

"Of course. Many people wish to conduct their business privately."

"Excellent. And do you know of firms in town importing cotton from India?"

"Would you require a Glasgow firm, ma'am?" Only when he said it for the first time did Orla realize he wasn't in the habit of Mr. McNary to call her madam or ma'am at every turn. She liked him.

"Well, I would prefer it. Is that more difficult to find or risky to support than London?"

"There are some in Glasgow, but the large affairs would be in London and Liverpool. If you like, I can draw up a short list of those I might recommend? We can discuss the merits of each at our next meeting."

"I see. Yes, that would be appreciated."

He nodded and made a note in the ledger open on his desk.

"Would you be able to give me your opinion of my plan, Mr. Grant? Is it likely to be a steady income?"

He paused and tapped a finger on the page. "The port will tell you where most ships are coming from, and the politics of that place may indicate whether it will be profitable to buy and whether it is likely to continue doing so. I don't suppose you would like to be always buying and selling, constantly shifting your shares, would you, Mrs. Smith?"

"No, you are correct. I would want a good going concern where I can be a staunch supporter. If I decide to split off more of my annuity to buy joint stock, I may try another concern, however. It will depend on the news—politics, as you say."

His eyes gleamed and she caught a glimpse of his excitement about something. She had no earthly idea what it might be. Politics?

"I do not like to take chances," she admitted. "But I would like to know my income is not going to support slave plantations."

"Is this why you specified India and not the West Indian cotton that is more prevalent here?"

She nodded. "Or that from the Americas, which is the same." She took a deep breath and looked him full in the face, this mild-mannered, bourgeois-seeming solicitor. "My husband was a minister of God. The money he left me came from the Church. I want to be a good steward of it, both for my own livelihood, and perhaps—" her voice lost its steady volume and her gaze fell to her lap, "—perhaps help the Reform cause."

She waited a few moments to hear his reaction but no sigh or scraping of a chair leg alerted her to his thoughts. She looked up to find him smiling slightly, that gleam in his eyes only brighter.

"Well," he said, almost breathless. "That is singularly fortifying to hear, Mrs. Smith. Have you then, talked with Mr. McNary about the unstamped press?"

"Oh, yes!" She answered his excitement with eagerness. "I subscribe to one or two of the papers and he told me only last week that he himself puts out a weekly!"

He joined her to chuckle at their friend's modesty. "Yes, our Mr. McNary can keep most things about himself snug under wraps, can't he."

They spoke a little more about her newly discovered delights, and the solicitor took down the details of the London man to write and have it all changed over so he could execute her requests in cotton import firms. Orla left feeling more cheered and competent than she had since her husband first took ill.

As this was the evening she had invited the sisters Arbischer for supper, she hurried back to go through her chores and make her cottage as homely as could be. She'd got a very good leg of lamb from the butcher, and diligently went to work cutting potatoes for a baked dish with cheese that she knew was a favorite with them. It was the perfect time for gooseberries, so she procured these from a road-seller on her way back as well.

They didn't warm to her little tabby beast immediately, but as he stayed well-behaved, Orla hoped they might get used to each other in time. She brought each woman a small glass of sherry in the parlor before they sat at her pitifully small table where the food lay cooling.

"Betsy tells me you've been hithering and thithering since you've been back from your travels," said Mrs. Lockhaven.

"No doubt it is a good deal of business to keep you in and out of Town so much," Miss Arbischer added, fishing for details.

She sipped from her own small glass before answering. The village gossips. She must learn more from them than they from her.

"No more than the usual financial questions, I'm afraid. I'm changing solicitors to one up here, that is all."

Miss Arbischer's eyebrows rose while her sister nodded understandingly.

"It is a lot to take up when one is not used to it," she agreed. "But it will become second nature in time, dear Mrs. Smith. We're just so glad your husband was prudent about your accommodations, so you could stay right here with us in the village. I can't imagine this house went for nothing, and he must have been paying it off for such a long time!"

The realization of such timing and planning had not dawned on her before, and she felt a new pang of gratitude toward Robert, which brought tears to her eyes. A handkerchief appeared in front of her averted gaze and she sniffled into it a moment before regaining her composure. "Thank you," she whispered.

"It is a good thing such a deep-feeling woman as you are hasn't been preyed upon by that new neighbor, Mrs. Smith," confided Miss Arbischer. "We've heard of his paying visits to all the mamas of marriageable misses in the villages round, but never any one twice."

"Oh, that Mr. Tate will find someone obliging, don't you worry, Betsy. Obliging to the family business *and* with a dowry, I'm sure those are his requirements, with any connections merely icing on the cake. Although there is many a man out here who did very well for himself before, it's not like it was."

A hush fell over the conversation. Orla waited a moment before standing and gesturing for them to be seated at the table.

Chapter 11

Next Monday it would be July; this week, all the gentlefolk from London were rusticating on their estates, and soon there would be parties of them passing through Glasgow on their way to hunting lodges. Orla was reading about the trend in one of her weeklies, where the practice was described as part of a 'hegemonic display of exclusivity that leads only to starvation of the many in need.'

Well, as long as they turn a blind eye to a bit of poaching, Orla thought, *we should be all right.* She stopped herself with that 'we,' as she realized it had been several years since she could count herself among 'the many in need.' She still had trouble letting go of thinking like her father did.

She still remembered the day when her husband had a second curacy added, bringing their income up to forty pounds a year—riches! The day after it happened there had been a dray accident with one of the parishioners, and Orla had consoled with the poor widow, while one of the local gentry had quietly taken control of the situation to arrange for funerary expenses and an annuity. That was supposed to have been her responsibility, she was stingingly told afterwards. But no one told her where the line was. It seemed it was constantly shifting, and with it, society's expectation of her did, too.

But never mind those old memories of not measuring up: something exciting would be taking place on Friday. After all her haphazard lessons with friends in the south, she'd gone and paid money for lessons from a real music teacher! Her first lesson would be with a Mrs. Crenshawe who lived in a cottage similar to her own in Paisley. The rector's wife had kindly offered their carriage for the ride of six miles each Friday, as a way to exercise their older gelding, who was retired as her husband's riding horse. That should help her think more like a settled and comfortable widow.

She'd written in response to Mrs. Crenshawe's advertisement in the Glasgow Observer and liked her candid reply. She expected a lady with good sense, but when she stepped out of the carriage, what she beheld was just on this side of eccentric. Mrs. Crenshawe stood in her doorway, a stern expression on her face showing all her sixty-odd years, and several long layers of gauze floating in the teasing wind around her form.

The lady seemed to want to preserve the look of the fine muslins from fifteen years ago, but had added the buttressing warmth of sturdy petticoats underneath, thank goodness. Orla allowed a smile to soften her face as she reached out a hand to say hello. At first, no hand was forthcoming. The lady peered at her with small eyes before relaxing and stiffly offering a timid squeeze of her fingers as greeting.

"Let's go in, no sense standing in the street for everybody to gawk at."

Orla followed her inside. Straight from the street, the door opened onto a large-ish double room. The front window let in a good amount of light, so that she could see a sparsely furnished parlor. On the left end stood the pianoforte, and on the opposite end was the fireplace, which held no fire, it being a fine summery day.

"Now, you wrote that you were a complete novice. No instruction whatsoever?"

"None, ma'am."

"Well, perhaps that will work in your favor, since you have formed no bad habits. Can you sing, Mrs. Smith?"

"Sing? Er—"

The woman put her through her paces with a couple of church hymns, doing them backward and in double time to test her natural ability. Then the lady told her to copy how Mrs. Crenshawe sung, which she was fairly certain was never going to happen. Then she was finally bade to sit down and take a breath. She spent the next hour hearing notes and having them pointed out to her on a treble clef, a few faint lines on a paper. By the end, Orla's eyes were straining to see any dots or blotches, and her ears were sorely confused.

"Right. Next time we continue in the same vein. Adieu!"

She was shuttled out of the parlor and felt her feet hit the street without ceremony. She was about to feel indignant when she realized she was doing something she'd wanted to for so long, she couldn't possibly find fault with it. Next week would be a different story.

After being dropped at the rector's stable, she walked home with a bounce in her step, humming abstractly and trying to retain the sound of her instructor's voice on her ear. She entered her cottage to see the cat on the windowsill, tail swishing.

"You can't be up to anything good, looking like that," she said to him.

A knock on the door made her turn in surprise. It was the boy from the neighboring cottage, a few hundred feet to the south.

"Mrs. Smith! They told me I was to give you a message as soon as you arrived home. I just heard your door so I came running as fast as I could—"

"Wait a minute, Jemmy," she said, holding in a laugh. "That was quicker than I hardly got in myself. Well done. What's the message?"

He held out his hand, which contained a crumpled sheet of finely textured paper.

"Thank you, Jemmy. Good lad."

He disappeared with a clatter of feet on the stone stoop. Orla sighed. An urgent message? *Who could have urgent business with me?* The possibilities made her heart sink: her brother, about her father, or her new solicitor, about the portfolio change.

Once she smoothed it out, it was apparent it was from the solicitor, Mr. Grant.

Dear Mrs. Smith,

I trust I find you well. I thought it prudent to inform you that an ill-advised and possibly malicious sale of your capital stock has been initiated. I was informed and am trying to remedy the case. Would appreciate your speedy reply and if you are available, your presence in my office Saturday morning when I will have a notary present to take testimony as notary. Cordially Yours,

Mr. Jerm^e Grant, Esq.

That was tomorrow morning. She wrote at the bottom of his note that she would be there, addressed it again, and hustled to the butcher's to have the messenger boy deliver it to the receiving house. With luck he would get her reply by the late mail.

With luck? That did not seem to be the operating conditions, she admitted, before shutting her door and proceeding with her afternoon chores. Too many questions intruded on her peace, and she passed a broken night in bed.

By the next morning, she was so keyed up that the cat must have sensed all was not well. He spent a quarter of an hour yowling at her in bed, then disappearing when she finally climbed out. One more bad sign she did not need. She made her way to the cab stand, humped and bumped her way into town, and walked with mounting dread to the modest office in Threadneedle Street.

It was yet early enough that the office door was not open. Orla turned back to the street in desperation. *Drat! Now where can I wait for him?* She hadn't realized it was not yet nine o'clock. Only half past eight, she judged. Just as she was about to sacrifice a few coins to sit in a coffeehouse, she saw Mr. Grant rounding the corner, his morning coat swirling in the wind from the main road.

"Mrs. Smith! I say, you are prompt. Come in," he said, as he unlocked the door and ushered her in.

"Your letter was most unsettling, I could hardly fail to be here at my earliest opportunity."

"I am sorry to have to upset you. But I thought it best to act as swiftly as we might. There are a couple of options. Come in, sit down."

He hung up his coat and stowed his carry-all while she sank carefully onto the wide-bottomed chair in front of his desk.

"It's like this," he started in. "I sent the notice to this Gittlings right away when you asked a fortnight ago. It should take no more than a week for him to have sent up everything from your accounts. I thought to start the proceedings with the cotton shares last week when it was settled, but instead of a gentlemanly reply from him, I had to ask the director of Coutts' branch here why it was taking so long, and he informed me that the shares under your name had in fact been sold in an order from the previous week. He did not recognize the fellow's name turning over the bona fides, but remembered it because it stuck out, and therefore showed this to me when I inquired whether he'd heard aught of this man Gittlings." He sighed after this lengthy explanation.

"He sold them at a good price, of course. And now there is no way to re-acquire them without paying the difference, which is substantial."

"But," stammered Orla, "where is the money from the sale of the shares? Surely that is mine?"

"It is," Grant replied with a strained tone. "It is set up in an account with my name on it, as was supposed to have been done, but as a deposit rather than a security. And less the profit from the premium price."

"What does that mean?"

"Effectively, you are starting out again with the nominal value from your husband's purchased shares. About four hundred pounds in total. It's not nothing, by any means, but if you want to buy back those shares for a regular income, you would have to pay the current premium, which is set at 30 per cent."

Orla opened her mouth to speak and came out with nothing.

"But he's a swindler! Where do we report him?"

"That is one path to follow, to be sure, but I very much fear this man would have taken steps to call into question his own guilt and intent." His eyes softened. "It seems he bore you no small amount of ill will. I am sorry."

"So we are not likely to pin the blame on him." Grant shook his head. "What is our other option?" Her voice sounded raspy, as if her throat were readying for the barrage of tears it knew would come.

"Your chosen cotton ventures, while we haven't taken any yet, have done very well in the last week. You could simply move in that direction with all your capital, instead of the 5% you proposed."

Her jaw dropped open again. "But isn't that very risky speculation?"

He canted his head one way then the other. "It would be very solid in the right hands. Now I know we've only started a working relationship, Mrs. Smith, so you may want to check the references yourself. I wouldn't blame you at all, but this firm is the one I would recommend. I am completely disinterested in its business, aside from observing their scrupulous practices and dependable shipments in season. If I had a sister, I would suggest the very same to her," he finished.

Orla sat back in the seat, trying to catch her breath. She wanted to believe him but was there a wiser choice?

"May I see the references?"

He handed her a paper and she saw four names and addresses listed on it. The third one made her eyes go a bit blurry.

"These seem unimpeachable, I suppose. May I write to them?"

"Of course. I'll have the clerk we use make a copy for you. He's usually here a few minutes after me."

"Thank you. And—" Orla paused, trying to be wise, and cautious. "You wouldn't recommend dividing a portion of the deposit into the consol, and a portion into the cotton importers'?"

That would be Darcy's recommendation, she thought. She wondered at Grant's leaping at this chance. Was he perhaps not as disinterested a spectator as he said?

"That would be a prudent approach to regaining the capital you've lost. Safer, surely, but you would likely have to retrench in some areas." He winced, as if he knew how simply she already lived.

"Do you suppose the rise in the cotton import shares to be quick, then? Or of long duration? It can't be both, or more people would be jumping at the chance and the price would go up, no?"

"It would, which is why I think buying now would avail you much better than later. However you settled upon the commodity, it was a lucky draw, for two reasons, Mrs. Smith. It has just capitalized and the initial shares almost distributed and there is a favorable law expected to go through regarding the trade with India within the month. That is the rest of the reason I would say time is of the essence."

"I see, of course. I will call upon the references," she trembled as she said it. "And then be able to tell you for certain on Monday, if that would be enough time to effect the trade?"

"I hope so, ma'am."

She bit her lip. "All right. Then I suppose I have some business to see to!" She said it with a watery smile. There was a noise at the outer door.

"Richardson! I need you to make a copy now, please!" Grant called. A young clerk with shaggy black hair and a high brow came in. He handed the clerk the page of references and gestured to Orla. "She'll be waiting for you, so this first, please."

"Yes, sir," the young man grabbed the page, pulling an arm out from his jacket as he hurriedly got to work. While she waited, Grant asked her about the lending library and whether she'd been to any of the lectures hosted by McNary's weekly.

"Lectures? No! Why must I hear about his exploits from you always?" She asked with a laugh. "First his own paper, and now a lecture series...tell me, what is it about?"

They chatted comfortably about her reading and the turnpike parade for the few minutes it took the clerk to write out a copy. Once he returned, Orla stood and thanked them both, then hurried away to visit at least two of these references which might decide her future.

Chapter 12

Mr. James Ewing.

Most recent Lord Provost of Glasgow and current Member of Parliament.

Would he be here in Glasgow while Parliament was sitting? She had no notion how the Members lived and conducted their duties, but she knew Parliament was meeting and passing Acts by the reading of her weeklies.

But she knew where she would be informed of his whereabouts: the Bank of Glasgow, which he'd helped create. Where her money stood. Where the supposed mix-up had been recorded. Where there would be no punishment for Mr. Gittlings.

She strode to the Bank to try to speak to someone before they took an early lunch. Something told her anyone important who would know Mr. Ewing's location would be the type of man who would take an early lunch. She was proven right, but arrived most auspiciously at a time when Mr. Ewing was wrapping up a meeting with the Director. So the teller informed her when he came back down, assuring her it would only be a short wait.

So he does travel while Parliament is in session. Interesting. She filed that information away, along with uncomfortable memories of the last time she'd seen Mr. Ewing's daughter.

When Orla had first been married, Robert had been assigned to a rural parish in Dunoon and Kilmun, where she had met the daughter of the very wealthy West Indian merchant by chance doing errands. She and Jane had become slight friends, and it didn't develop further because much was expected of the daughter of James Ewing. One didn't want to be tainted with low associations.

The last time she had seen Jane was at Robert's funeral. When Orla had been moving around the country, they'd kept in slight touch, but only when she was widowed did Jane, now long married, show her face. Jane—Mrs. Crum now—spoke to her stiffly, and Orla was aware of the three children who accompanied her: stiff in their own finery, peering at such a curious, plain woman in mourning, no doubt wondering why their mother took notice of her.

Orla shook her head of the memory of the Ewings' treatment and gave her name to the teller. She watched as he ascended the stairs to the mezzanine, where the important man's desk sat, surveying all. She looked firmly away as he was told of her request. A quarter of an hour later, her patience was rewarded when a thick-set, powerfully built man looked down on her from under beetled brows.

"Mrs. Smith, it isn't Mrs. Smith of Crookston?"

He had recognized her after all.

"Yes, sir. I am flattered you remember me, it has been such a long time."

The great man nodded at the teller, who melted away. He gestured for her to retake her seat in front of the teller's desk, borrowed for the moment, and seated himself.

"Not at all. I hope you and the minister are doing well—that is—" Too late his eyes glanced down to her violet gown and registered it was possibly her half-mourning.

"Robert died last year, Mr. Ewing."

"I'm so sorry, Mrs. Smith."

"It was sudden. It was a wrench. I'm doing well enough now. But I came to you for a reference, regarding a firm I am considering investing in."

His eyebrows shot up, and his spine stiffened the slightest bit. "Is that so? Well, I am glad to hear you are comfortable enough to be choosy. I wouldn't want to think of my Sara's old friend struggling along. Now, which firm are you looking at?"

"Oswald, Stevenson, & Co."

"Ah! Well, I can recommend them without reservation. Oswald is a canny man, and Stevenson is an inventor, the sharpest of a good lot. They are doing well with their own concern in Barrowfield, and trading with the East India states when they are allowed."

He gave her a brief smile, and she wondered at it. A passing reference to his chagrin, or amusement at some situation in the East Indies?

"When they are allowed?" she sought to clarify.

"Oh, the EIC, you know, tries to gobble up everything for King and Crown. But merchants do get in a deal or two. I'd say that is a profoundly safe investment. I'm impressed you came here to find me for a reference. Good timing, eh? Normally I'd be down in London and you'd've had to write."

"Yes," she said faintly. She cleared her throat, wanting to project authority. "And their trading partners don't disappear? And their shareholders stand by them?"

"I should say so. I'm one of them, though there are few enough of us at the moment." He eyed her speculatively. Perhaps wondering if she'd been tipped off by someone he knew. "Well, as lovely as this surprise visit has been, I really must be going along to all my appointments in Town, Mrs. Smith."

"Of course, I'm glad to have caught you for a moment."

"Not at all. And my deepest sympathies, again."

She bowed her head and allowed him time to rise and depart. After he was gone, she did the same herself, her heart setting a faster pace than usual.

The other reference was a wholesaling draper who did business with the cotton importers. He also had nothing but good things to say about the firm. Orla returned home with questions forming, and she wrote them down so as not to forget when she retraced her steps to Mr. Grant's office on Monday. In the meantime, she had a call to return on the Arbischer sisters.

They dined early at six o'clock, and the fare was simple. Orla was glad of their familiar bickering; it made her smile, when all the uncertainties of her future would have made her pull at her own hair. She didn't share her worries, as that would have been to invite the trouble into their house. Instead, they talked of the village goings-on.

"A butcher's daughter! Just think," Louise was saying.

Betsy tsked into her wine. "I think she does well. We all know marriage is the only way for a woman to advance her social position, short of—well, the only respectable way."

"Or inheriting," Louise added.

"Yes, but that is likely to be known, and counted on. It already forms a picture of her fortunes. Not many are *surprised* by an inheritance. That is the stuff of novels, Louise."

"More are surprised by the lack of one, I'm sure," Orla said.

The sisters nodded. Betsy helped herself to another portion of pickled onions. "How is that cat of yours doing? Causing any new mischief?"

Orla shook her head. "He is not, and I am thankful. He is such a good companion. Maybe I should find a kitten for Isobel. She might like a little company, too."

She sensed the quick glance between the women and her heart stuttered. "What is it?"

"You haven't heard the news about your friend yet?"

"No, what's happened?"

"It seems she's engaged to that Mr. Tate who bought up the old Abernathy property a few months ago."

"Oh! Well, that's—that must be good news—the best of news!—for her. She was just telling me she was ready to consider marriage again."

Betsy eyed her for a moment then put down her wine. "Do you think she will change her friends?" she asked softly.

"No," Orla said loyally, but wondered if this were what made her heart stutter. She'd been friends with Isobel since they were both married, and their visits had been mostly light gossip and pleasure outings. Would she leave her out of her new life, on the arm of someone who socialized with a viscount?

"No," she repeated. "I'm sure she will be as kind and attentive as ever," she said more softly. "Now, would either of you fancy attending a lecture on the unstamped press with me in Renfield Street on Friday?"

It was an enjoyable visit, but Orla was pleased at the end of the summer night to see her cottage in the twilight, two eyes reflecting the last rays of the sun from her window. She let herself in and tidied up for the night. She sat in her chair then, listening to the night-cooling sounds, and hoped for a good outcome on Monday. She did not wish to have to revert to dependency on a man so quickly.

Chapter 13

The meeting with Mr. Grant on Monday proceeded as she had envisioned. Her questions about timing and records and banking were answered from the reports he had compiled on the firm on his own time. Everything added up. She signed the papers to empower him to purchase in her name, as should have been necessary for Gittlings to sell in her name—but it wouldn't do to keep harping on a past ill, she reminded herself.

Now it remained only to watch the Oswald, Stevenson, & Co. firm like a hawk and keep her ears open for news. And perhaps pay a wise woman for a charm…but that was her old father's way. She decided to visit her brother and father the next week. She already had enough to juggle between the piano lesson and the lecture she'd committed to attend with Betsy on Wednesday. She'd already paid the money to the music teacher for six lessons, and the lecture was free. Orla had enjoyed her brief respite from worrying about every shilling and penny.

She arrived to collect Mrs. Lockhaven at four o'clock, a little dismayed at the impeded state of her readiness when she peeked in. Betsy stood with Orla in the front room while Louise went to and fro, remembering one article, neglecting another, until finally she was ready to venture out.

"Goodness! What a sorry state to be in," she said apologetically to Orla as they left Betsy on the step. Orla shared a smile with the sister waving from the door and assured her it was all fine. They caught the stagecoach for Town and alighted in Argyle Street, then marched up Union Street for the editorial offices of two newspapers. The top floor was something of a bar, with one long counter on one side, and many chairs and tables, the latter of which were pushed to the counter to make more room.

"The first issue is the secondary right," a flushed young man was saying as they entered. "We have the right to educate ourselves, and distribute without crippling fees!"

"Aye, aye!" came the cry from several throats around them. It was mostly men, but she spotted two ladies sitting amongst them. She had a sudden urge to know them, these potential allies, but had no pretext for an introduction, and anyway, the man was speaking. Orla guided Louise to a chair on the periphery, one of the few that was left open, and stood nearby to listen.

"The primary issue is ending the rich man's protectionist tariffs on corn! How are we to recompense the laborers in the factories, how are they to feed their families? With the prices so high, it is no wonder desperation and despair lead so many to crime to survive!"

He went on in this vein, a trifle fond of his own voice, Orla thought. But after a few minutes, he finished, and a calmer-looking gentleman succeeded him in the speaker's corner.

"Is he *Black*?" whispered Louise.

The man was only thirty or so feet away and the top floor afforded them dusky light from many windows, so it was abundantly clear that Mrs. Lockhaven was correct. The man's complexion was light but assuredly his face bore the signs of African heritage and his hair the same: a wide nose and the tightly curled dark hair that were usually only seen in livery in front of the great houses in Glasgow.

"The Repeal of the Corn Laws is a noble cause, I am here to agree with it." A round of applause greeted this visitor. "But I am here with an even nobler one: the recognition of humanity in our Enslaved Brethren in Servitude, in chains, in fetters, in Hell."

He ended his opening gambit in a grave, soft voice, and there was no censoring of his speech, but a collective leaning in to hear him.

"I have heard some say that freed slaves have received a fairer bargain than the white 'wage slaves' here in the northern cities." He gave a meaningful glance to a far corner of the room, and Orla followed his gaze to find a red-haired gentleman with a skeptical brow raised in response.

"While there are many trials the two groups share in common: lack of alternatives, local monopolies, no redress in the courts, no public relief for their situation; at least the white man does not have a constant fear of being snatched up in the street and forced to give over his life's work, his labors and health, for another man without a say. Or his children's lives! And even if this does not occur to a man, the fear of it can invite the white man to turn tyrant for his own gain. It is too easy."

"Not since the pressgangs stopped, anyway," came a shout from the other side of the room. Orla wondered about pressgangs. Her brother had been just barely too young for the wars with France, hadn't he? Or had he gone round with the fear of being snatched for a cabin boy? And was that now a thing of the past? Her heart recoiled a little from the horror of imagining it. But the man was speaking again.

"Ah, but that is the Government's doing! And a different case again, for it may happen to us as well. But one man to merely say the word, and have another man in chains, with no wrongdoing, no rumor, no excuse, no court, no sentence—just what his parentage has stamped on his skin.

"Should not the press be treating these evils as vociferously as the Corn Laws? Or no, since habit has long made enslavement and exploitation an uncomfortable but necessary evil for the Empire to continue? Speak of that, it is another argument for your radical reform in enfranchisement, for there also is an evil that the Empire needs to continue to maintain control."

The room was silent now, no jibes thrown at him. Orla suddenly realized it was because he could be considered as committing treason with such seditious talk against the state. She held her breath, wondering if someone would call him out. The red-haired man who had looked so skeptical rose and heads turned when the creak of his chair groaned in the silence. The danger of the moment made the nape of her neck prickle with unease.

"The worthy gentleman speaks of an honorable cause. Liberty is what they called for in France, and we thought smugly to have seized it without a struggle here over a century ago. Well," he made a noise half cough and half disbelieving laugh. "Mr. Cuffey will no doubt expound upon how we may combine our Unstamped agitation with that of the Abolitionists without risking sending good men to the crowded jails."

Eager exhalations changed the atmosphere from unease to interest, and Orla felt the power this man's one small correction had exerted. She glanced at Louise, rapt at the speech now flowing out of this man Cuffey's mouth. Orla half-turned to the gentleman standing next to her.

"Excuse me, do you know that gentleman's name, in the corner?"

"That'd be James Bronterre O'Brien, ma'am. Writer at a paper or two, like," he replied in a hushed voice.

She thanked him and listened keenly.

The ride home in the hansom was slow but she welcomed it. Louise's interest has been roused as well, and they repeated the allusions made that they had not understood, trying to remember them long enough to search out answers on their own. Orla may have doubted her spinster neighbor's experience, but she was quickly coming to appreciate her nimble mind.

Chapter 14

The piano lesson that week had been difficult. When she had been berated at the first lesson, Orla had risen to the challenge, not wanting to cower at the first clash of wills. But this had been an hour of pure heckling. Her posture, her comprehension, her very hands were addressed with contempt as lacking and irredeemable. She had departed feeling beaten down like old iron in the forge, the smith trying to make something new, and failing.

She went into Town to try and cheer herself. It wasn't the time for the lending library to be open, but she passed by it anyway, pausing on the pavement opposite to let her eye run over its plain, solid features. The door opened and she blinked. It was the same red-haired man from the lecture she'd attended two days ago!

He walked briskly away, looking neither left nor right, adjusting his coat sleeve as he went. Orla's gaze slowly turned back to the door. It was shut again. But was it Mr. McNary he'd been in to see? She didn't know the other business the library conducted, or that McNary himself conducted, but she would certainly pose some pointed questions to him at their next meeting. If only she could walk up and knock on that door...

but no, it was not her business. And it was not important, merely curiosity.

Intense curiosity.

That O'Brien from a few days ago had been a wily crowd manipulator, no doubt about that. But it had been helpful, in the event. She wondered what else he got up to, in other lectures.

Well, I shall have to attend more of them to find out. The thought gave her a little glow of warmth, of purpose that had been missing after the disastrous session with the harping Mrs. Crenshawe.

The next week her visits to her brother and father were due, and Orla was girding herself mentally for the encounter. She'd done fairly well at putting her financial precarity out of her mind, so there was no reason she could not do the same with past nastiness or present uncaring and salvage what she could from the relationship. That's what she told herself as she knocked on her father's door, anyway.

Olive answered it again. How much time did the girl spend at her grandfather's?

"Hello, Olive. Are you officially the greeter for the house?"

Olive gave her a queer look then wiped it from her face, stepping back so she could enter the dark space.

"Is Father upstairs again?"

"Aye, he's havin' a wee kip," she answered shortly.

"Are Elspeth and the children about?"

"They're out marketing," she said.

Why so tight-lipped? Orla wondered. "I see. I'll go up and see if he's awake. I can walk back to the inn with you if not, if that's all right with you?"

She got a shrug in response. She put down her coat, hat, and purse before venturing up the stairs. It was somewhat brighter in the upper room, but also close with the summer heat. She saw her father's long body on top of the bedsheets and heard his breath whistling out of his nose. Quietly she sat on the top step and regarded the room.

Plain wood with gaps in the floorboards. Bits of damp evident in the plaster walls. Murky glass in the windows that had not been cleaned for some time. But also: brightly colored rag rugs and quilts covering both beds, scrubbed-clean hearth tiles, and a mug of fresh wildflowers on the dresser next to the bed her father slept in. It was a picture of someone struggling to find beauty in life, and endeared Orla to the wife who had been none too welcoming on her first visit.

She snuck back down and gave Olive a shake of her head. The girl was edgy, fidgeting and giving her sidelong looks that she couldn't guess at.

"Now, Olive," she began. The girl cut in.

"He's ill again, and Ma is blaming that late-night vigil at the church for your soul. Not to mention the extra pennies we gave up at collection. She—she's—"

"Hold on to yourself a moment, Olive. Before we get into assigning blame, what's the illness? Is it something serious?"

"We don't know," the girl said in a smaller voice. "Doctor hasn't come since we called him last night."

"Has he been sleeping since last night?" A note of alarm crept into her voice. It was almost tea time.

"Just about. Ma says he were awake a couple hours before dawn, but didn't move around, like." Orla noticed the intensifying accent but didn't bother remonstrating with a daughter clearly in distress.

It didn't sound like the apoplexy that had carried off her husband, but it could very well be something serious. Her father would never have spent a day abed when she was growing up.

"Are your mother and sister really out marketing?" Orla held her breath.

"Aye, they left me to look after 'im and wait for the doctor."

She let out the breath in a long, controlled exhale. *Damn the wildflowers, they should have gone for the doctor.*

"I'm just going to go back up to check on him, and then I'll head over to my brother's place. He should know someone to send if the man here is occupied. All right?"

The dark, straight hair showed a clean part as the girl nodded and kept her head down.

"Don't you worry, we'll find help." She didn't want to promise more than that.

Olive looked miserable, but Orla didn't think it was in her power to alleviate that hurt, so she squeezed her shoulder gently and picked up her things once again.

By the time she arrived at Christopher's pub, her worry and her fast, anxious pace had wilted all the starch in her clothing. She had no time for elaborate pleasantries.

"Mrs. Rafferty?" She addressed the woman washing and drying glasses and cutlery meticulously behind the bar. She turned round: a pleasingly rounded face and figure and blondish brown hair in ringlets.

"Yes?"

"I'm Christopher's sister. Orla. I sent a note, but there's a rather pressing—"

"Oh, yes. Nice to meet you."

"Of course—I mean, nice to meet you as well. Where is my brother?"

"Oh, he's about the place, sure enough. We were expecting you for supper, indeed, but you're a touch early…"

"Yes, I called in at my father's and it appears he is ill. I wanted to ask Christopher for the doctor in the neighborhood, or the next best thing."

"What would that be, a nurse? A veterinary?"

Orla sighed explosively but held her tongue. When Christopher had said a general-at-arms he had not mentioned Serena was one to wear down her opponents with slow, measured questions.

Feeling the exasperated shout about to leap forth from her throat, Orla turned on her heel and looked into the stable block, the yard, the scullery—though why her brother would be in that little outhouse, she couldn't say. She was tempted to simply shout his name from the yard, so frustrated was she at the inhospitality she was receiving, but then he appeared.

"Orla, I can hear your temper from all the way over here, what is it?"

He was rounding the corner by the front door, so apparently he had not been in, but visiting.

"Where were you?" she asked, stung by his temper comment, though it was spot on.

"Just seeing a man about a horse."

"Ah. Father's caught something. Last night. The doctor hasn't come, and he's been asleep nearly all day. Do you know someone who could help?"

His soft gaze sharpened at the news, her tension communicating to him the urgency.

"I do. If he's...yes, I'll go for Dr. Clements."

"It's almost busy hour, isn't it? Can I help Serena here?"

He scoffed. "I doubt it much, Mrs. Smith, that you know how to serve as barmaid?" When Orla opened her mouth with nothing to say, he smirked. "Just sit tight. I'll find Dr. Clements, see to Father, and let you know what I find out."

"Thank you," she said, feeling truly grateful, both for the knowledge and action as well as the unburdening of responsibility from Olive's shoulders.

"Your wee room above the parlor is made up for you," Christopher said, before hurrying off to the stables.

Chapter 15

Orla sat on the bed, ruminating about the turn of her fortunes in the past weeks. What had Olive meant by the vigil for her soul? Would the new investment turn out to be better, worse, or the same in terms of her income? Was she a fool to trust to these new friends she'd made since her widowhood? Who else *was* there, in truth!

While such morose thoughts flitted through her mind, she stared at the well-swept but small fireplace. No fires needed in July. No heavy woollens. Her gaze unfocused, she drifted into a sort of trance, her thoughts mercifully arrested, but the feeling that something was about to be revealed caused a maddening tickling sensation.

A bark of laughter broke Orla from her meditation, or whatever depths she had dropped into. She listened, brow creased into a frown. A party had moved into the private parlor below and she could hear them speaking.

"Again?"

She sighed in exasperation. *Just when I was in need of the rest.* But then her ears pricked at the sound of the voices: ones whose cadences she recognized from her visit the month before. *Could this be the same group?*

She once again crept closer to the cupboard and opened its doors to hear where their words were clearest.

"…clear as day. It's going to come to a head."

"But now or ten years from now, Charles? None of us can wait that long! The vein of gold in cotton is gone."

The voices were recognizable from her last overnight visit, especially as they were discussing the same topic. She wondered if she'd be in for another round of late night ribald jokes. *But it seems something has changed*, Orla thought. *They don't sound like they are in a jesting mood.* It must be the same group of cotton importers as last month. Orla kept silent and strained her ears.

"…twenty years from now! Borrow what you need to stay open and switch gradually, then, Cully."

"…my name, and you know it."

A beat of silence, then, low and strong: "We must be the making of the firm so they will not stray." Two more voices joined in agreement.

"…men are dragging as it is. Mine are loyal but there's only so much a man of worth can take, Ormond."

The names without context were confusing but she tried to remember every word so she could make sense of it later.

"…revolt, so we get the orders in any way we must. Call it the luxury version, then explain it's a new product by the same artisans. I don't care, so long as it's done!"

The angry words were followed by more objections and argument. Orla's breath starting coming in little gasps involuntarily. When the conversation passed on to Parliament matters and London gossip, she finally took a deep breath in relief. She hurried to her purse and found a sheaf of papers she could write on the back of, recording all the words, names, and accusations she had heard and felt from the voices. When she was done, she sat back on her heels on the floor, wondering if she had a solid lead or whether she would be throwing good money after bad to follow overheard advice yet again. But no— the cotton firms she'd found were doing well. She could trust these men, if they were the same. Better check with her brother.

She took a small meal at the bar, going down to break the ice with Serena while giving a quick nonchalant glance at the group beyond the doorway in the private parlor. Serena caught her looking. She gestured with her chin as she put together the plate of pickled beef and potatoes with bread for her supper.

"What ye after with them?"

Orla turned back around. "Nothing, just wondering who they were." Then after a moment, she lowered her voice and leaned closer to her sister-in-law. "I can hear their conversation up in my room, I suppose you know?"

"Oh, aye."

"They're saying some interesting things."

"Are they? The fusty old cloth merchants? Could've fooled me." Serena gave her a smile that seemed to invite confidences. Perhaps they were sharing a secret, their first since Serena's marriage to Christopher over a decade ago.

"Do you know their names? Do they meet here regularly?" Orla asked in a whisper.

Serena had to welcome a few new people coming in for a pint, then returned. "They meet regular, third Saturday, and pay to reserve the parlor in advance. Not many do, so we snap it up."

Orla nodded. "And who pays?"

"Under what name, you mean?" Serena smiled lop-sidedly, as if it was obvious that high-minded folk would disguise a secret meeting. "Ormond. It's a foreign enough one, so I can remember."

So that had been someone's real name. The name clicked into place in her memory, to ask Mr. McNary about later. "Thank you, Serena. And thank you for supper. I'm sorry to deprive you of your husband for the rush."

But as she looked around, she realized it wasn't as busy as she had anticipated.

Serena concurred. "Not so bad," she said with a shrug. "I do hope your father is on the mend. I know you may have had your own difficulties with the man, but he's a decent one."

Orla wanted to reach for her arm to acknowledge the kindness, but still felt that was too intimate for this second visit. Her anxiety for her father showed in her eyes though, as she looked back and nodded.

She returned to her room with the tray and sat to think her way through her options. She stared at that empty fire-place for at least an hour, the remains of her supper congealing in cloudy drops of butter and grease. A knock on the stout door claimed her attention from her dreamy imaginings.

"Yes," she said clearly. The door opened inward and Christopher stood framed in it.

"It's cholera." His eyes were bloodshot and his hair was mussed. His clothes, comfortably worn a few hours before, now looked dusty and decrepit with hard use.

"Christopher! The girls? His wife?"

"They're under quarantine, but—"

"Olive?"

"—Clements wanted to keep you as well, but...I suspect Olive lied to him and said neither you nor she had been in the house."

Orla covered her mouth with her hand. A creeping dread had taken hold in her belly. And the piercing pathos of that girl trying to shield her from their fate.

"Oh, Christopher. Is there a new outbreak? Or is it just their house?"

"Just their house, and one the next street over. Clements is doing a thorough search still."

"It isn't of necessity fatal," Orla reminded herself. Reminded them both.

"No," her brother admitted. "But he is getting on in years. It's...taken him bad now."

A harsh cry tore from her throat. "This is not how I wanted to —"

"I know." Her brother stepped hesitantly into the room and opened up his arms to her. She hadn't cried since the first month after her husband's passing, and not in her brother's hearing since they were children. But sobbing into his shoulder now felt right and natural.

It was over quickly, a storm blowing through her, but it had been a blessed relief. She gathered herself and said a prayer that her father's young family would not be laid low by this terrible disease. Then she ducked her head further and said a prayer that she hadn't brought the infection to this home.

She lifted her head slowly, her hands on Christopher's arms. Sniffled.

"I'll do what I can, and keep you informed. You'd better go home tomorrow. Perhaps stay home."

"I will. And send replies, of course."

He nodded. She squeezed his arms before dropping her grip.

"Good night, Chris."

"Good night, sis."

Chapter 16

Orla spent three days at home, wringing her hands, waiting for symptoms to sprout, and news to come, but there was nothing. Saturday's note from her brother said her father was just as bad, but none of the family had succumbed. Sunday's note said the same again.

She went through her stores of flour and eggs and milk, half convinced she felt weak, and half-berating herself for her imagined maladies. She was drinking a cup of water shakily on the evening of the third day when the latest note came with the post. Before opening it, Orla sent up another prayer for her father.

Sister,

Our father seems to have broken through the worst. He is very weak and in bad condition but enough rest and good broth will slowly restore him, the doctor says. Doctor Clements has been very busy in the neighborhood. Eleven houses were struck. But only three have died. He says it is a weak strain, thank the Lord. The other side of town seems to have it worse. Sadie seems to have gone through a mild case, but her mother and sister were not affected. Please return your reply affirming your continued good health and I shall be,

Gratefully Yours,
Christopher Rafferty

So. She could breathe again. She went out to the privy, which had been difficult in her waiting state, and observed no ill effects except those of her nervous stomach. She proceeded with a cold cloth to perform her ablutions, trying to wipe away her worries as well.

Her first errand was to send a reply to her brother. That done, she headed straight for the butcher's for the staple items she'd run out of. She counted out her pence and had a moment of doubt as to her financial position then shooed that away. *One dreadful turn at a time,* she warned her internal accountant.

Monday—she had missed her usual day to see Mr. McNary at the library. It was too late in the day to drive in now. She sighed and settled into evening chores. She used the time making rolls for the morning to calm herself and give thanks that her father was not gone, that her chance for a relationship with him again was not denied.

She was just shaping the rolls and placing them in the basket to proof when a knock sounded at her door. It was past tea-time. She glanced out the window, seeing the late July sun still hanging above the horizon. A frisson stole over her arms. *No, not—*

"Mr. McNary?"

The small, neat man stood half facing away from her. At her voice he turned and his eyes lit up.

"Ah, Mrs. Smith! I am sorry to call so late, it is only that I was worried when you did not appear during the library's hours as usual."

"No, I—" She glanced around at the lane and weighed up public opinion against her gratitude at his thoughtfulness. He had come on a fine bay horse, who was currently munching on the grass of her front garden. "No, of course. I am sorry to give you cause to worry. Please come in."

She stepped back to allow him passage and hoped no one happened to pass while his horse was out front.

When they were seated, she explained. "We have only had a dreadful upset about my father, over in Rutherglen?" He nodded. "I've just received a note from my brother that he is finally recovering, but I didn't want to leave until I knew, and in case I…"

"Quite," Mr. McNary agreed. "I'm sorry to hear of his illness. I know it was even worse in the spring, over in Paisley."

"I wasn't going out then much either," she said wryly.

"Of course."

After a pause, she asked, "Did something happen at the library today? Is there something you wanted to see me about, in particular?"

"Ah, well…in fact, there is a new push for subscriptions to supplement the Unstamped Papers. A friend of mine is undertaking to write for the cause in his own paper, and I thought you might be interested to help."

Orla's interest sharpened. "Would this be a Mr. O'Brien?"

McNary looked surprised. "Yes. Do you know him?"

"I only heard him speak a few times at a lecture. He makes quite an impression."

McNary chuckled. "He does that. He can not help it with that booming voice of his. But he has a good heart, and I think will be able to rouse many of our miners and spinners to the cause."

Booming voice? Orla had only heard him speak with grave, measured tones. Still, he had made an impression. And this must have been why she saw him leave the library last week. She wished she could volunteer right then.

"Mr. McNary, before my father took ill, I also had a blow on my own account. I won't trouble you with details, just to say that my financial state is precarious at present. I am due to talk with your Mr. Grant again next week, and we hope for good news. But I must not commit more resources until I know my own fate."

During her quiet admission, McNary had flinched, straightening in his seat. He leaned forward, as if wanting to reach for her hand. Orla curled her hands together in her lap, trying not to twist the fabric of her skirt in her now-sweaty grip. Should she not have mentioned it?

But the man smoothly settled back, allowing his face alone to show he grieved for her troubles.

"I am truly sorry, Mrs. Smith. If there is anything I can do—"
Of course there was not, but she sighed at his words. They were kind.

"I will come back on Friday for my next books," she assured him. "As my subscription does not run out until Michaelmas. But until I meet with Mr. Grant, I must hold off any other purchases."

"I understand. And I wish your father well." He stood up to make his way out when they both turned with surprise to a fresh knock at the door.

What? Another late caller? No, don't let it be—

Orla hurried to the door, forgetting her guest, only to find Isobel, wide-eyed and wondering, on her step. Her carriage stood in the lane, and McNary's horse stood nickering with Isobel's beasts in harness.

Orla let out a breath and it turned into laughter, she was so relieved. Isobel didn't take it well.

"I come by to see how you're faring on my way home and—"
She stopped abruptly as her eyes shifted behind Orla. She turned to see Mr. McNary executing a small bow.

"Mrs. Foxton, may I present Mr. McNary, of the library on Threadneedle Street. Mr. McNary, Mrs. Foxton, one of my esteemed friends in Crookston."

Isobel had her mouth gaping open, as if she couldn't decide what to say first. Mr. McNary saved her.

"A pleasure to make your acquaintance, Mrs. Foxton."

"But I am *not* Mrs. Foxton," she cried. "That is what I have come to tell you, Orla. I—" But she stopped, unsure whether to go on in the presence of this interloper.

Mr. McNary took the hint and excused himself, taking his horse off directly. Isobel turned to her friend with eyes like saucers.

"A gentleman friend, Orla? At this hour?"

"It is complicated, Isobel. But out with your news first! Are you married again?"

She finally closed her mouth, then let it spread back into a grin. "Yes, and my new name, can you guess it?"

Orla took a deep breath to overcome the sinking feeling in her stomach. "Tate?"

Isobel squealed. "Yes! How did you know? Though I suppose the neighborhood has been alive with the news this past week."

"Indeed, no. Or perhaps—I do not know. I haven't been…It was the sisters that told me it might be forthcoming." Isobel peered at her as she stuttered.

"All right, what has happened? What have I missed? Why is my news not the happy banner it should be?"

"Oh, it is only a right series of shocks to the system. My father fell ill." At her friend's raised eyebrows and quick grasp of her wrist, Orla continued. "Thank you. He should be able to recover, but it was the cholera—Rutherglen is lucky to have lost so few. I was worrying about that, and whether I had contracted it, so I haven't been among the village for the past few days. No cause for alarm on my account, but I've only just heard about his recovery, so Mr. McNary came unannounced, worried at my not showing at my usual time. And then I had to tell—"

"Is he so attentive, this gentleman? What is his family?"

Orla blinked, surprised. "I have no idea. No, he is simply the manager, or the owner, I don't know, of the lending library. I know they do some other business, perhaps a press, but—"

"A tradesman? Well. Then it was rather presumptuous of him."

"It was kind, Isobel, that is all. Do not tell me you are getting airs, now that you are married to an earl's son. We have always valued kindness here."

"True." She sat in silence a long moment. "Well. I'm afraid I must get home—soon I will be in the new home, you know, that my husband is building. For us. I am very happy. I am sorry—well, I must be getting back. Good night."

They kissed goodbye and she waved from her carriage. Her own carriage. Orla felt a strange shift had occurred in their relationship. She remembered walking in, practically unannounced, to her rooms three months before. And now? She suspected the delicate lady would not be at home if she came to call. An ache of sorrow replaced her relief at her father turning the corner and her pleasure at being fussed over by Mr. McNary. So many shocks to the system tonight.

She went over her evening tasks slowly, not seeing. And when she woke, it was to a quiet house.

Chapter 17

She took another day to recover from the emotional toll. Her father, McNary, her friend, the money—it all made her head feel like a cracked egg.

She still had several days to wait before going to see Mr. Grant about the new stock performance. But she could read up on the firm she had invested in. She pulled out the national newspaper she'd bought at the butcher's and settled herself at the table for a perusal.

His lordship the feline chose that moment to jump through the high window and she jumped back up, knocking over her cup of milk.

"No, no! Oh—" Now she was out the milk *and* the paper. She glared at the cat and took a shaky breath. "This isn't starting out any better of a day."

The cat did not deign to look up, instead licking its lifted paw. Orla grunted in frustration and went to fetch a cloth. She cleaned up the floor and wrung out the cloth. It was her last one, so she would need to deliver up her basket of laundry to the dairy, where Martha took in washing. She would take stock of her cottage and her accounts.

"Not as if there will be the parade of people from last night, so at least we won't be disturbed."

She beheld the chaos of her parlor. Sighing, Orla gritted her teeth and dove into the fray, moving from one side of the room to the other, marshaling her focus for each task. At the end of twenty minutes, she was satisfied with the level of tidiness. The cat had stayed well out of her bustling way during the whirligig, atop the table. She came back, much calmer in spirit, to give him a pat, and noticed some discarded papers.

Looking into their folded depths, she realized what they were: her notes of the overheard conversations at Christopher's, from before she'd learned the extent of of her father's illness. As she read them over, the picture in her imagination—that of a swindle about to be sprung—took shape. There were pieces she did not understand, about switching over and borrowing, and having loyal men, but the phrase, 'a new product by the same artisans' certainly had her senses buzzing.

Now—Ormond. It was he whom she needed to identify. Serena had called them cloth merchants. Did that mean drapers? Or import and export agents? It sounded as if they were cloth importers, one of the many firms along the river Clyde dealing in textiles from abroad. Would her new firm perhaps know them?

Orla's knees trembled at the thought of her capital being entrusted to a partner in a swindle. Well, she would find out what she could. Starting with a visit to Mr. McNary.

When she arrived at the library the next day, it was just after luncheon and not yet open. Still, she rang the bell and listened for a response. After a long minute, the door swung in and she saw an elderly face in a crumpled suit. The man was blinking at her, clearly surprised to see anyone.

"I'm sorry for intruding, Mr.—" Thankfully, he supplied his name.

"Treliss, madam." *Oh, no, not the madams again.*

"Mr. Treliss, thank you. I was hoping to speak to Mr. McNary for a moment, if he was in?"

"Nay, madam. Out a-visiting. Shall I take him your card?"

"Yes, that's—a good thought." She struggled to get her cards out from her purse, which was holding rather too many things at the moment. "There. And I'll come round again before I return home, in case I can catch him. It is quite important."

"Yes, madam, I'll see he gets it."

That done, she consulted her hastily sketched map of where the firm was situated, and after orienting herself, set off at a brisk pace to find a hansom.

Oswald, Stevenson, & Co. had its main office close by the Linthouse estate, a neighborhood she was unfamiliar with. She arrived at the edge of the estate, and passed through the break in the great, gray wall to walk the hot, dusty way to what she assumed was the management building, as it stood guarding the way to the more elegant edifice beyond. It also gave onto a street running directly to the Clyde, where she could see masts towering above the few buildings and mature treetops.

Remembering her mission, she readied her appeal speech and tapped the knocker on the door. It sprang open and she was soon subject to a shocked inspection of her person by a balding, middle-aged clerk. She could tell by his ink-stained fingers and hunched posture that he must be one of the junior clerks, despite his age.

"Ma'am?" He said blankly, clearly at a loss as to what she could want there.

"Good day. Are Mr. Oswald and Mr. Stevenson in?" *Start with the bravado.*

"Ah, no. But the manager is here, do you have an appointment with the directors?" He looked doubtful.

"No, but I'll see the manager for a moment, if I could."

Orla gave her name, knowing it would mean nothing, and stood patiently while the man ran off, leaving the door open. It was a typical agent's office, with multiple desks full of clerks, all busily writing contracts. A doorway showed the way to inventory, and through to the higher echelons of the company. She restrained herself to wandering eyes only, not wanting to miss the chance to speak with the manager.

She got it. Orla was ushered into a spartan office and introduced to Mr. Fanway. She got right to the point once the clerk had left. After the introductions, he started probing for her bona fides.

"I have in mind to invest in this firm, but I had heard a rumor about an unsavory individual that you might have had dealings with. I wanted to assure myself that he is unconnected with your operations before instructing my agent to invest."

She spoke low, since the open door was required for her 'feminine virtue.' She didn't want anyone else to hear her outrageous yarns.

"What is this individual's name?" Fanway asked.

"A Mr. Ormond." She observed his reaction closely. His jaw closed in reflex, making his neck appear fatter. At the same time, his eyes, which had seemed bored if obliging, had retreated, til they looked as dull as lead slugs.

"There is an Ormond who owns a spinning mill a few miles upriver. He may buy some of our goods from wholesalers but we have no control over who they sell to." His eyes narrowed and Orla resisted the urge to swallow. "Do you know what this man was being accused of, to be labeled as 'unsavory'?"

"I believe it has to do with cheating in his sales."

The manager's eyebrows shot up. "And who has passed you this information that you trust?"

Orla lifted her chin. "I would prefer not to say. You understand."

His manner became brusque and professional again. "Well, I can not assure you of the man's business practices, as his customers are not mine. But I have not heard any bad said of him, since he's worked in the neighborhood, and in any event, we don't do any direct business with him. I hope that is satisfactory to assuage your doubts and fears."

She noted the lack of address. She had just poked a hornet's nest, if her sixth sense was correct, and so knew she had to withdraw immediately. She nodded to him.

"Thank you for seeing me, Mr. Fanway."

"Mrs. Smith." Was that the tiniest bit of derision in his tone? She walked out with her head high.

Completely for show. As soon as she reached the end of the long road and was out of sight she slumped against the grey wall and pulled off her gloves with shaky hands. She wet a handkerchief with her eau de vie and held it against her throat for a long moment, willing herself to calm.

There was a fox in the henhouse. Now she had to investigate whether it was the lowly manager or whether he was receiving orders from on high. And for this she would need help. She set off in the direction she had come, eventually finding a cab.

She must have looked quite flustered when she arrived back at the library, for Mr. McNary ushered her in with a look of concern. He sat her down by his desk in the back and quickly fetched a glass of cool water for her. After the initial surprise at her divulged confidences, he sat across from her and listened to her deductions. No one else was in the library, except the elderly man, who looked to be sleeping on burlap sacks by the window.

"So you wanted to see if the firm you have invested in was connected with the skullduggery you overheard at your brother's pub," McNary was saying slowly. "And now you think the manager may be in league with one of the schemers?"

Before Orla could launch into her several possible theories, someone knocked and the porter woke up to go see to the door.

"It is because he mentioned swapping—or switching—one good for another and calling a luxury—"

She stopped in confusion, for the red-headed man from the lectures had come up to meet them.

"O'Brien," said McNary, rising to grasp his hand. "I've been wanting you to meet my dear Mrs. Smith. Mrs. Smith, Mr. Bronterre O'Brien, editor of the Poor Man's Guardian and several others, I imagine." This was said with a conspiratorial, a collegial, smile. Orla felt like the rug had been pulled from under her feet. She had urgent confidential information to share. What was McNary doing?

They got their niceties over with and O'Brien pulled a chair over, his familiarity with the furniture not escaping her notice.

"I have wanted to introduce you for some time now, as compatriots working for similar aims."

"Ah yes, I hear we are to have some gold sprinkled into our coffers to offset the stamp duties—" McNary was shaking his head. "No?"

"Not quite. I'm afraid she's more akin to us church mice than I had thought." McNary shared an easy smile. Orla was becoming silently furious, such that her neck was feeling quite hot.

"What you gentlemen may consider a topic for jest is a matter of some moment to my future. I would appreciate if my financial status was not bandied about as if I were not sitting here," she said as frostily as she could manage.

"I do beg your pardon," said McNary, looking surprised that she had neither understood nor appreciated his humor.

"Excuse my friend, Mrs. Smith. We are all of us in straitened circumstances from one month to the next. Well. If you are not to be our new donor, I have at least seen you at a lecture. And with a friend! Converting to the cause already—that I must admire."

"There were several causes that day, Mr. O'Brien," she replied. "And I'm not sure I could say that the Plight of the Unstamped won out in terms of magnitude."

"Fair enough. But you are not in a position to buy any slaves their freedom or make Parliament alter its laws, are you, Mrs. Smith? So what shall you do while you wait? That is the mark of wisdom."

He waited for her answer while she wanted to slap his smug face. *How had this turning to a friend become a hostile boxing ring today? Haven't I enough to deal with?*

Still he waited for an answer.

"I hear there is a campaign of petitions," she said in a low voice, unsure to trust whether she would not shout at the man.

"Indeed, and when you know a woman's signature is not much good for that endeavor?"

"James, come now—"

"The women of any movement can speak, and arm themselves, and gather intelligence, Mr. O'Brien. Something it seems your platform currently lacks."

Finally she had the satisfaction of seeing his face change: from lax coyness to alert resentment. McNary tried again to intervene.

"This is not what I had hoped to accomplish by bringing you together. I fear it has been a long day and we may be hasty in —"

"It has been an exceedingly long day, Mr. McNary," she agreed. "I would appreciate speaking to you for a moment alone."

O'Brien made an elaborate show of rising and sauntering to the window.

"I want advice, Mr. McNary." He gestured for her to continue. "The firm does seem to entertain a working relationship with this Ormond fellow, and I do believe they are planning some sort of swindle, which I prefer not to be party to!" she whispered fiercely.

"But the money is already gone to buy shares, and I can not change the order with Mr. Grant without giving away my knowledge—my *suspicion*—of their wrongdoing. I wondered if you had any knowledge of the cloth merchants, the wholesalers, this Ormond, the Oswald firm—anything that could help me know which is foul and which fair." She looked him earnestly in the face.

"We do have a sort of board of journalists," he said evasively. "Like Mr. O'Brien here, others of us meet to discuss political issues and such, and there is one intimate with the textile imports and another who may know about the drapers. They cover their industries for the papers, you understand?"

"Yes," she said eagerly. "And can you get a word to them easily?"

"We are due to meet this evening, in fact. I am one of them; I cover the books." He gave a sheepish smile.

"You write about the publishers?"

"Yes, though under a pseudonym."

"Are you that shy about it?"

"Well, you know..."

"I shouldn't be. I think it's marvelous."

"Well! I'm glad."

"So, tonight?"

Mr. McNary seemed to collect himself after the small revelation. He blinked.

"Yes, of course. I could bring you the news after, but it will be quite late, and I wouldn't want to encounter another of your neighbors..."

"No...I am sorry about that." Orla thought rapidly. "I will go back to my brother's. I may be presuming too much, but I feel this is keenly important. I'll be back first thing in the morning to hear your news, and decide what to do." She stood abruptly.

"Thank you, Mr. McNary." She turned to the taller man at the window and raised her voice. "Mr. O'Brien. Good evening."

He bowed from the waist as she sailed out the door, and was banished forthwith from her thoughts.

Chapter 18

Her brother was surprised to see her again so soon, but made room for her in one of the children's trundle beds. She supped with Serena and the children, as her brother manned the bar.

She was awake the next morning at five, and quickly dressed, moving quietly among the children. As she passed their eldest daughter going out to the stable, she was struck by the quiet of the house, the coolness of the air, which during the day was so hot and thick with manure. She and Olive stole a moment together in the kitchen before Serena started the fire. Bread, butter, and cheese were sliced and put away again amid conspiratorial glances. It made Orla feel part of the family again. Amid all the other uncertainties, she was grateful for it.

The light was strong when she set out for the library, opting again not to pay for a hansom. She attempted to walk with a slow, measured pace so as not to arrive mussed, but the humidity made her clothes cling to her skin in a most indecorous manner. She paused to fluff her skirt about for a tiny bit of relief and sank onto a stone parapet for several moments to let her skin cool.

As she was sitting, she observed the working folk on their own paths, most heading toward the river, thence to the shipyards or the mills on the edges of the city. They reminded her of an ant army, tromping along the city streets like a modern forest floor. She thought about the places they were marching to, the ones she'd read about in her papers, and that made her start chewing her lip.

Orla started walking again at a more determined pace. She thought about the Oswald firm, what it did business in, and the wholesalers and drapers who depended on them. By the time she was face-to-face with a tired-looking McNary, she had the bones of a plan.

The slight man struggled with an air of embarrassment still.

"He really is a good friend, it's just the timing, but—"

"I'm sure you're right, Mr. McNary, but I haven't time for new friends' feelings at present. I'm sure Mr. O'Brien can be brusque when he needs to be; allow me the same privilege."

McNary closed his gaping mouth.

"Tell me the news."

They sat just inside the door, the porter giving the back of the floor a casual mop. *Really, I'm surprised this place appeared clean to me.* McNary told her of the textile reporter, with news of the East India Company's difficulties, and then of the shopkeepers reporter, who had relayed news of the larger draper's emporia and their advertising changes. Orla stared at her gloved hands, her mind sorting through the bones of her plan, fleshing them out with muscle and sinew.

When McNary was finished, he looked at her questioningly.

"What will you do?"

"I have one more day before I must meet Mr. Grant, and I will be ready." She said it to sound confident, but wasn't sure if the man was fooled.

"To think, you walked in here a few months ago, knowing nothing of the market," he said in wonder. "What stirred you up so? Why go to the meetings and read all the latest headlines?"

"I would have remained ignorant if not for the treachery of men," she replied. "And I am only doing my best to provide for myself with the knowledge to hand. I am grateful to you for your help, Mr. McNary. You do know that?" He nodded. "Well, then. I'll be off home."

"Did you want the day's paper?"

She turned from the doorknob to smile. "Oh, yes. Might as well."

"You may have changed what went into it, so yes, you might," returned a smiling McNary, as he handed her the pristine sheets. She folded it into her reticule.

"Much obliged, sir."

The day went by slowly at home. Hot and sultry for a British day, full of battling insects and hungry birds swooping down. Orla, after a refreshingly cold sponge-bath, decided to call on the sisters. She found Betsy reading a novel and Louise writing letters. Both put down what they were doing to enquire after her night visitor, for the whole street had heard by now.

"He is a kind friend who was worried when I failed to keep an appointment. I have been ever so faithful at the library. It appears he also hosts a reporters' meeting or society, or some such, I have just learned. It is very interesting."

"But is he married?" Mrs. Lockhaven interjected.

"Oh, I should think so. I've never asked," replied Orla.

Miss Arbischer sighed. "I told you, Louise. Not interested."

"Well, after that friend of yours taking up with Mr. Tate, and hearing of your financial woes, I couldn't be certain…"

"Let me put both your minds at rest. Yes, there was a financial…miscommunication, but I am setting that right with the help of my solicitor. I hope I may say I'm coming out of it a more knowledgeable investor."

The look on Betsy's face suggested she didn't think that was a positive. Orla grinned.

"And I mean to expose a certain person's trickery. Is that good enough for you? But it's a secret, so don't tell."

That achieved the desired effect: much interest and promised discretion.

"If ever you have advice about the consols, we wouldn't tell a soul," Louise confided seriously.

"Oh, I have nothing to do with that," she said, laughing. "This is merely a very specific matter of a dockside company. It shall be sorted, I shall put my money situation right, and those who were trying to pull the wool over our eyes will find it's not wool at all..." She almost laughed but pressed her lips together. "And that's all I can say. I should be going now for the post."

She bid them good day and picked up the two letters left for her at the butcher's, one from her niece Olive. It was a halting and laborious letter of gratitude mixed with pride and well wishes and news of Lennán's weakened-but-hopeful state. It was quite a muddle, all in all, but Orla clutched it to her chest, satisfied to be drawing at least one member of that household closer.

She spent her evening alone with the cat, thinking through her theories and sipping her way through many cups of tea.

The next morning she presented herself at Grant's office like normal. He greeted her like normal, if a tad anxious.

"Tell me, please. Don't draw it out," she said immediately when his pinched brows drew together.

"Mrs. Smith. Good morning. It is only the earliest of news, but it looks to be favorable. In any event, you can't sell back now until after the bank holiday, but the last quarter's report lists..." He rattled off some indicators that he thought she would find comforting. She did not find them so. Her stern face again drew his anxious brows.

"That is what you were seeking, was it not? A safe place for your capital?"

"Only I have fallen into a bit of investigating, and it does not seem safe after all, for the hopeful signs are based on lying and disguising. The rumors from India are that the rare cotton is done for—typhoons or mob rule, take your pick, but something has laid waste to the region where all the finest artisans worked. It's gone. And they're sending us lower quality but calling it a new luxury product. I don't know how they convinced the mills to pay the same for it, because it can't be the same to work with, but for the customer at the counter, it will be inferior goods for the same price, labeled as high quality at a discount. You follow?"

"Erm, yes, but how did you—"

"Nevermind how I discovered all this. The favorable indicators you just quoted me mean that the importers, Oswald et al., have forced everyone else to go along with them. But they can't forever, and I want to be out before they take that step." She paused. "I also want to show the public their lies."

"After the fact."

"Yes."

The man sat with that for a moment, and Orla squirmed inwardly. If she could have called attention to their behavior before without losing herself her widow's income, she would, but as it was, a week's worth of fabric or more might go out and spoil someone's inventory before she could act. Or perhaps there would be many uses for the new cotton; who knew?

"I know what it looks like, but it is the best I can do in the circumstances." Mr. Grant looked up from his ruminating and nodded slowly.

"I only want to be sure you are in a safe position when you throw out an accusation like that. I will need to do some research and prepare. You have one week at least before you intend to change your stocks again?"

"At least," she agreed.

"Very well. We are in agreement."

They discussed several contingency plans, and when Grant knew her preferences, he sat back in his seat with a sad sigh.

"McNary said your father was ill?"

"Oh, thank you for asking. He is much wasted from the illness, but recovering now. I will wait another day or two more to see him. My brother has had the care of him at the Tabby—the Fighting Tabby, that is, their inn. I am only recently reacquainted with the family." She ducked her head, embarrassed to be airing family business.

"Well, that is to the good. I am recently reacquainted with a branch of my family as well. It doesn't do to lose people. In Scotland, with our hills, you may never find them again!"

He chuckled. She smiled in reply but said nothing. Her split family was all over the island, and back in Ireland, and across the seas. There was little hope of reuniting it now.

Chapter 19

Time to retrench Dream Number Two, Orla thought grimly. Not that she minded much, as brittle as Mrs. Crenshawe's temper was. She wouldn't regret the few weeks of lessons she had suffered through, for now she had some things to practice next time she visited her friends' grand houses, at least. So, it hadn't been for nothing.

The display of pique when Mrs. Crenshawe was informed of her discontinuing the lessons, though, that was definitely unwarranted.

And it was as she suspected with Isobel. She regretted her friend's changed behavior, but didn't particularly blame her friend for it. She had met and known Isobel through the years when she and Robert had been at their most successful; she had never bared her soul to the woman about her childhood and family tragedies. She was only too sure most people in Scotland would be deaf to cries for pity from an Irish family. The religious and social prejudice was too strong; that was why she had converted, though her father hadn't understood.

All this long history stretched before Orla as she sat with her secrets that week, hoping for news: of her father's recovery, of the firm's contracts with the government being renewed, and of their new ships landing safely.

When all three messages had reached her, it was mid-August, and harvest time. She was putting up the brambles for jam when she heard a knock at the door. Thinking it was one of the sisters or the butcher's boy, she called, "It's open!" For she couldn't be bothered, with her hands stained with juice and the pot set to boil over.

The door swung inward slowly and she saw first the copper head of the man, then his hat in hand as he peered into the dark recesses of the cottage.

"Mr. O'Brien?" Orla was astonished. "I—I'm sorry, do come in. I'll be with you in a moment. I just—"

"No, don't be sorry. I come without notice. Do not be disturbed; nothing is wrong with McNary. I merely extracted your direction from him so I could come pay a call. Sorry to arrive in the middle of..." His gaze fell to her busy hands and the glass jars, most standing half-full.

"Just a moment," she said again, feeling wretchedly bedraggled. She topped up the jars with paraffin from the smaller pot and deftly attached the lids. Ignoring the detritus from the mashing and sieving, she rolled down her sleeves and swiped a few tendrils of hair back behind her ears. "Now," she said finally. "Won't you sit down."

His sneaking smile rather annoyed her, but she reminded herself to be hospitable. *What are you bloody doing here?* she wanted to ask.

"I suppose you're wondering why I turned up?"

She turned a sweet smile on him, which showed him exactly what she was thinking.

"Ha! Well, you've good reason to wonder. I last left you with a jeer and a taunt and I wanted to apologize. McNary and I go back rather a long way and he defends your good sense and initiative and thinks you would in fact be helpful with the Unstamped campaigns."

"You still sound doubtful."

"I have an open mind," he said, his hands opening to indicate his generosity. "And what is more, an open schedule—at the moment. Mr. McNary, however much he would like to help, does not. I thought that offering mutual aid might be a better start than…I did not mean to insult you, Mrs. Smith. I want to help you if I can."

He sat back, waiting for her to pass judgment, decide whether he was worthy of being let in to her secret as McNary had been. She observed his large forehead, his deep-set eyes, his small, thick lips. He did seem rather full of himself, but that was something she had observed in many men. He'd shown himself diplomatic in that lecture at an awkward moment. He'd shown himself presumptuous at their first meeting at the library. She closed her eyes. *That red hair, though.*

Meeting his gaze again, she asked him, "What is your first desire in life?"

He returned her serious look.

"Irish liberty," he said.

Her eyes fell to the floor. "Irish liberty, so a repeal of the Union. A Repeal, so Reform. Reform, so popular agitation. Popular agitation—through the newspapers."

"Yes."

"Do you stop often on your crusade to help those in distress, Mr. O'Brien?"

"As often as I can."

"Then it is not a straight, fast road?"

"No. A muddy track, indeed." He smiled a little at the racetrack reference, and she joined him.

"All right." And she explained her plan with Grant. He asked her about the contingencies, and she informed him of their intentions.

"It is not without risk, but I can not think of any better stratagem."

"Thank you for coming, Mr. O'Brien." They rose together and she saw him out. He put his hat back on and walked away. She rolled her sleeves back up and put more fuel on the fire.

Her father had left his bed, her brother wrote her to say. The small wave of cholera in Rutherglen seemed to have stopped before the city had to bear down on the neighborhood. Custom had briefly wavered at the tavern, but was now back to its usual clamor. Orla was glad for them. She would visit again, and bring gifts if she could, in September. For now, she was going in to Town three times a week to pursue inquiries.

The firm had remained untouched; no rumor disturbed its trade. Grant had made the move to sell her shares and distribute the realized profit and capital among four other firms she'd found and vetted. She had just met with the wife of the last firm's manager and they'd gone for an ice. This firm was enjoying solid business and the manager's wife thought Orla was an important client to woo. Orla did not want to deprive her of her good humor and eager fussing.

They were chatting in the window of the sweet shop when a man stopped on the pavement. As they were both observing the street, neither of them could help noticing him. His face went livid and he rushed into the shop.

"You! You're the spy; I saw you at the the Tabby!" He was staring straight at Orla.

She didn't recognize the man and felt horrified and embarrassed that he was causing such a scene. But her brother's tavern…all the other customers had stopped their own conversation and looked over.

"I've never seen you before in my life," she said, even though she could feel the triteness of the assertion as she said it. She tried for a little more force: "I don't know what you're talking about. You must be mad." He grabbed her wrist and raised it, shaking her whole arm. His face was florid and she began to worry not only for herself but that he really was mad and might hurt someone, or himself. "Sir, please, I think you're thinking of someone else."

Finally, someone came to restrain him. She touched her wrist immediately, relieved, until she saw whom it was. Mr. O'Brien stood by the florid jackanapes, speaking to the man quickly in a low voice. O'Brien tugged at his jacket, as if he'd just done an unpleasant task and would wash his hands of it. The florid accuser now looked ashen-faced and almost ran into the door before pulling it open and escaping into the August afternoon.

Her guest the manager's wife was similarly ashen. "What was that about?" she half-whispered.

"I haven't the faintest clue," Orla offered, somewhat truthfully. Who could have seen her and connected any events now happening with that meeting on which she'd eavesdropped more than a month ago? "But I am glad Mr. O'Brien happened to be nearby when he did." She rubbed her wrist gingerly while she turned to make introductions.

After such a disruption, the women agreed to part ways for the day. O'Brien politely bid the woman farewell and waited to escort Orla home.

"How did you happen to be here?" she whispered as they walked to the cab stand.

"I told you I had an open schedule. I feared once you made your move something like this would happen. It will blow over, but the tempers…I thought it might be prudent."

"A little more time in the mud?"

"Something like that."

"Well, thank you."

"Not at all."

He handed her into the cab and she left Town for Crookston a little earlier than expected. How had that angry man known? She supposed he was a cotton importer, one of the bunch who had been colluding in the room below. But how had he connected a stock share and an anonymous letter in the *Union Gazette* to her? To her face, even! Could it be Christopher…? She thought about it on the ride home, a peculiar anxiety curling tight around her insides.

Chapter 20

McNary

Oscar McNary sat at his desk, staring at the wall. The September meeting of their journalist set was that evening, so his mind kept paging through the issues to raise, rather than concentrating on the very trivial task of proofing the printer's order that sat on his desk. It was past the library's open hours, nearly nine o'clock when O'Brien and the others started trooping past him into the back room from the alley entrance.

The news reported that evening concerned hopeful achievements, denials from appeals, disappointing developments from the Honourables in Parliament, and changes in fortune in the various industries they covered in Glasgow. McNary attended closely, his other preoccupations forgotten for the moment as he strove to see the larger context these reports pointed to.

"And what about your wee project, McNary, your secret weapon?" Bludkin was asking.

"Secret what?"

"Your woman getting herself into trouble," he replied.

"Or us out of it," added Jamieson, to general laughter.

McNary winced. "In last month's meeting, I did disclose several pertinent facts, but that does not mean Mrs. Smith's business is anything to be bandied about." The hubbub quieted. "She is a gentlewoman with ideals and intelligence and I was well positioned to help her at a crucial moment. Now, the only way in which she will be spoken of in these proceedings is in the help she gives to the Unstamped press, do you hear? I expect she will be back at lectures and assisting the cause soon, and I very much hope if you shall meet with Mrs. Smith, you shall accord her the same respect you would to…"

He faltered, grasping for a figure these men would all venerate.

"—to the Princess Victoria!" Jamieson enjoined. He raised his tumbler of whisky high.

A few chuckles, a few raised glasses in response. McNary was relieved.

"Thank you, gentlemen. And now, if that is settled—"

"But we must hear how she fared," Bludkin interrupted. A few bolstering voices echoed him.

"Very well. The plan went on almost exactly as we wished. Grant sold her shares at a good profit after a week, Oswald did not suspect, as it was a small amount, and she found other places better suited, and shared out the capital. We then wrote the letter to the Working Men's Paper to insinuate the swindle she uncovered—thanks to you, Mr. Atkinson." More echoing cheers. "And they've had a bit of trouble selling ever since."

"And she's chosen well—what are the other firms?" asked Bludkin.

McNary met O'Brien's eyes, wanting to confirm whether that would be appropriate. O'Brien shook his head slightly.

"Well, that would be giving away trade secrets, wouldn't it?" Laughter answered him. "But yes, she's chosen well, and we wish her the best, and now are we concluded?"

"What about that stramash with O'Brien at the sweet shop? I heard about that," said a long-faced fellow named McLean. "How did one of the importers find her?"

O'Brien rose to quiet the burble of consternation that followed the remark. "Apparently some have not heard. Even though it is beside the business of this gathering, I will briefly report: the man McGillicuddy saw Mrs. Smith at a tavern where the blackguards met. He then saw her a month later when she went to inquire at the firm itself. He doesn't work there; it was simple bad luck that his memory was sharp for faces. But he is not ruined, so will not be so desperate as to strike out again. Only chastised. By me," he added with a grunt.

Another round of mumbled commentary made him add, "I told him it was our discovery, so he'd have to face the newspapers, not some lone investor. And he appeared to believe it. So."

McNary worried that they didn't have the full picture, but there wasn't much more they could do. He was uneasy with waiting out a dangerous commodity—someone vulnerable to blackmail—but very much wanted to believe that O'Brien had resolved the matter.

An accepting sort of quiet descended on the group and O'Brien sat down. He gave McNary the nod; the meeting went through its final motions and then men began swilling drinks and plunking them down with satisfaction. Thank you's drifted to McNary for the refreshment as they filed out, some after side-conversations. When the last had gone, O'Brien remained.

"Will she be all right?" McNary asked. He couldn't keep the edge of nervousness from his voice.

"Aye. She's a rare one. You may want her for the cause…"

McNary's eyes leapt to O'Brien. "Are you—"

O'Brien stopped him, flapping his hands at him. "I'm not anything, just a confounded bachelor who can see a gem for what it's worth." He looked at the ground, and McNary was on the point of venturing a consoling word when he spoke again. "Sure you can, too. 'S all right. I don't believe she's thinking about any of that now anyway."

McNary saw his brusque dismissal of the opening and abandoned his tack. A twinge of manly sympathy for the man sputtered under his ribs, but he only said, "No. Probably not."

"Well." O'Brien offered his hand to McNary; they shook. A point of honor. McNary understood he was to exercise his discretion about this man's concern for Mrs. Smith, but why did he not allow himself to hope for more than the slight acquaintance? McNary felt in the dark, but accepted that a man's heart could be closed even to a good friend.

"Godspeed."

Chapter 21

Christopher

He really was glad his sister was visiting now. The summer had taken on a slightly different quality with her as a new fixture. The scare with their father had been a wrench, but somehow having her to inform had made Christopher feel less alone. He should visit her in that cottage she had now, different from the manse he'd visited for the funeral breakfast. She seemed so competent now, less the unassuming girl he'd seen as the minister's wife, and more a woman able to stand on her own.

Christopher shook his head, wondering at it. Last time she'd visited, she'd even introduced Parliamentary matters at the supper table. He'd simply gaped, but his wife and some of the children had listened and asked questions. Children, in politics! What would she surprise him with next?

His wife was in the family parlor, looking over some receipts and grocers' bills. One of the children was in with her and he could hear their low conversation, interspersed with coaxing and exclamations in response. He swallowed hard, feeling how close they had come to being caught up in the outbreak from Orla visiting his father. She had started the ball rolling for the doctor; if that young wife of his father's had been in charge, the old man would probably be dead by now. Yes, he was glad Orla was back in their lives.

There was a bit of a commotion in the yard and he put down the laundry bill he was making double sure to come to the window and peer out. A fine carriage was just pulling to a halt, the matched blacks sporting shining leather and brass harnesses. He didn't recognize the insignia on the side of the carriage, but assumed it meant a peer was involved. The groom Fred was at the head of one horse already, good lad. The other groom Mack hovered around the door, waiting to be told to open it by the coachman, for he'd had a tongue-lashing for being too fast last week.

Finally, the door was opened, the step placed, and a woman in a very expensive lavender traveling ensemble stepped out, followed by a shrewd-looking gentleman in a dark suit. Christopher glanced down at his worn but passable dark coat and gray waistcoat. No visible stains. He was not built to play host to the quality, so he wasn't. He set his accounts under the counter and straightened up to receive the visitors.

"...I'd no idea," the lady was saying as she walked in the door held by her companion. "Perhaps he owns several."

"Good day, my lady," said Christopher. "How may we be of service?"

She'd stopped short. The gentleman behind her looked him up and down and raised an eyebrow. He finally spoke after a moment's deliberate pause.

"You are Mr. Rafferty." It wasn't posed as a question but he appeared to want confirmation, so Chris nodded. "And you have a sister, one Mrs. Smith."

Christopher felt his mouth flood with saliva. This would be an odd party to send if she were in trouble. Serena appeared in the doorway to the parlor. He shoo'ed her back, not wanting these people to see any more of his family, for they didn't seem particularly well disposed toward Orla.

"Aye. Do you have a message for her? From her?" he asked cautiously.

"No," continued the man, with a sniff. "We are…looking into an affair of hers." He smiled a nasty smile. Christopher swallowed. He didn't want to offend a peer, but neither did he want to put his sister in the wrong somehow.

"Well, then. Would you be wanting a pint or some wine while you go about your business, sir?"

"Oh, why not," he said. "I suppose it is close enough for an aperitif. Half a bottle of good claret for us." He looked around at the tables in the bar and directed his companion to a booth along the far wall. Christopher hurried to the door to the parlor.

Serena met him behind it, whispering furiously, "What do they want?"

"I don't know, something about Orla."

Serena's sharp intake of breath didn't help his frantic pulse. He hoped these people weren't the type to ruin a man's reputation for fun, but the man did seem officious and mean.

Christopher returned with the wine. A glance outside showed the grooms still had hold of the horses at the trough; so, they didn't mean to stay long. He ground his teeth at that.

At their table, the lady fixed him with her gaze. He put down the glasses and looked at her questioningly.

"We know you host the East India Company importers' guild each month. And we know that *Mrs. Smith*," she pronounced it slowly, with emphasis, "has been here, as well as several of their competitors' firms by the river, more than once. Would she be passing information along, confidential information? I wouldn't have thought it of her, but being alone can do strange things to one."

She leaned back to better be able to look down her nose at the standing proprietor. Christopher felt a powerful urge to defend his sister, and another to throttle this haughty woman, but held back both.

"My sister has visited me here a few times. Our father was recently ill. I know nothing about her business down by the river." And he didn't, for they didn't speak of such things when she stayed over.

"Is that so," stated the man; again, not a question. "I hope for your sake, and your family's, that nothing is found to contradict the truth of that. Some very important men lost a great amount of money last month, and so far, the finger points to her."

With great restraint, Christopher remained silent, knowing any more words might be twisted later. "Sir," he merely replied. He bowed and left their table to go back to the counter and his laundry bill, though his hands were trembling. The visitors sat alone in the tavern until a few men came in. They were artisans, if their highly individual clothing was anything to judge by. At once, the two troublemakers stood and processed out. Christopher held back from saying thank you or farewell. Who knew if they'd even left money to pay for their unfinished half bottle of expensive wine? He helped the men with their pints before going over to check.

A paper note for twice as much as the bottle was worth lay on the table. Well, at least the man had some honor. He pursed his lips. *That remains to be seen. The reference to 'my family's sake,'—that had not smacked of honor.*

Chris went about the normal evening business, brooding and stewing, trying to sort out an action to take that would do no harm. He decided upon calling on his sister the next day. Serena agreed when he told her; she would ask their neighbor at the junk shop to hang around to discourage any trouble. Uneasiness ruled their family supper, and Christopher wondered what Orla had got herself into.

Chapter 22

Tate

"What do you mean, closed? Then open it!"

Aloysius's normally perfectly-even temper was wearing so thin, he was shouting at menials now.

"But Mr. Tate, I can't open, I'm just the cleaner, you must wait for the manager—"

Aloysius reluctantly brandished a sovereign at the cringing creature. They stood outside the ticket office of a popular theatre.

"I need to meet with someone privately. They'll be here soon. Just let us into the theatre for a few minutes, no one has to know."

The battered man looked at the coin like it was hurting him. "I can't, I don't have the keys—"

"Oh, then of what use are you to me!" He turned away and marched round the corner from the ticket office to the front entrance. After looking both ways, he pounded on the large wooden door. He waited in an attitude of hope: hope that someone from inside the theatre would come, and hope that the person who was meeting him here would not.

Noise from inside. The sound of a barrier being lifted, if he was not mistaken. Yes!

"Good day, sir. Are you looking for someone from the company?" A large, dark-skinned man answered the door, blocking his way effectively with his frame and an outstretched hand on the open door.

"Oh, thank goodness! Why, yes, Miss Divina. She's not expecting me but she should be happy to see me."

Without commenting on his phrasing, the stagehand bowed and closed the door in his face.

Well, if he could rustle up an old paramour to arrange an empty room, all was not lost.

Several minutes later, the stagehand returned to usher him in. Tate gave another glance round to see if his counterpart had arrived, but he must have been delayed.

"I have another gentleman coming to see me here; he should be along presently. Please conduct him to us when he arrives."

"His name, sir?"

"Oswald."

Miss Divina was sleeping off a gin-soaked morning, but the stagehand stayed til he saw her start awake and smile at Tate; apparently that was enough of an encouragement, thank goodness. He left them alone in her dressing room.

"Aloysius, I told you you'd be back."

"I am here to meet another gentleman; you were a convenient excuse," he said brutally. She raised an eyebrow languidly, and he realized she was putting an entirely different construction on his words. "Not like that. He's in the neighborhood and we can't be seen together. This was the first place I thought of."

Her eyes softened. "Nice to know ye still think of me, pet."

He cleared his throat. "Is there another room, bigger? This one is in a shocking state."

Clothing was strewn everywhere, from floor to chair to globes for lamps. Bits of pink paper seemed to have been part of a general explosion. And Aloysius saw at least one broken glass hiding among the rubble.

"Oh, don't be like that. Fine, go along the hall to the backstage. That's an appropriate meeting place for conspirators."

His eyebrows shot up. "What makes you call us that?"

She looked at him with all the sarcasm and disdain he'd hurled at her. "I know you. But don't worry, I don't know his name." She waved a hand at him, the sleeve of her robe shredded. He almost asked what had happened, but remembered time was short.

"Thank you, Divina."

She closed her eyes and leant back upon the wall in the attitude he had found her.

He heard someone else coming in the hall and hurried out to meet them in the area where the ropes, pulleys, and sandbags stood behind stretched canvas scenery.

The stage rigger was coming, with Oswald behind, barely visible behind his guide.

"She said we should use the backstage. She's feeling indisposed."

Aloysius edged past the rigger, who eyed him narrowly before surveying the actress's room. When he saw that everything was as expected, he nodded and gestured the two men back along the hallway.

"It's on the left and down the stairs." The man shook his head, mystified by the ways of the fancy, and retired to his own office.

"Come, sir," said Aloysius. "We won't be disturbed." They made their way down the hall and then the long stair. Finally, they were in the quiet dark of the stage behind the curtain. "Careful, sir. There's rope about."

Two high windows gave scant light to see by, but Aloysius sat on a stool and watched as Oswald, gray-haired, bent, but looking sharp and shrewd, found a small chair.

"This is a nasty place. We should have gone to my club," were the first words he spoke.

"But you said—"

"I know, but this is degrading. Never mind. To business." He fixed Aloysius with his shrewd stare. "You owe me money."

"Yes, sir."

"And you lost me money."

"Yes, sir."

"You've just married but got no fortune from 'er."

"No, sir."

A silence that clearly contained the sentiment, 'then why the hell' stretched between them.

"How do you plan to repay me, then? Got strings to pull from daddy's estate?"

Aloysius chewed his lip, feeling an agony of mortification.

"Yes," he said shortly.

"Oh? When's that?"

Aloysius's mortification doubled at the eager, curious tone in the merchant's question. A man who was below him in rank, had started as a clerk, who had no connections at court— demanding satisfaction on his account!

"I collect the rents now. I can pay you back from that, if—"

"O-ho! So now we add embezzling to the gambling, won't Papa be proud!"

Only the knowledge that this man's underlings would find and beat him stopped Aloysius from wringing the man's neck in the shady reaches of the stage.

"The terms—"

"You're not in a position to negotiate now, Tate. The terms are you owe me thirteen hundred pounds from the past year's gaming, and your friend's treachery has cost us upwards of eighteen hundred more!"

"The weather and the political turmoil can not be laid—"

"He did not execute his task as ordered. No more must be said about it. Now, your father's estate…you collect what, a hundred quid per quarter?"

Oswald went on in vicious detail, evincing a familiarity with his father's affairs that the man himself would have been deeply offended and affronted by. Aloysius gulped. He wanted to defend his friend Toby, the captain who had come back with the first Company ship to be refused the Dhaka muslin, made to make do with an inferior product. He had already been stripped of his ship, for goodness' sake. Part—and only a small part, but part—of Aloysius's gaming had been in pursuit of some ready money to send to Toby, to make up for this same black mark. But most had been simple, desperate madness.

"What?" Oswald was quoting numbers at him so rapidly that they flew in one ear and out the other.

"Do you need these written down? Have you been struck dumb? No? Well, then. I'll expect the first three hundred pounds by the twentieth of October. Sterling. Don't try me." His sea-gray eyes flashed at Aloysius.

"But—"

"How does a man get out of this maze…" Oswald muttered as he strode away. Finding the stairs to the lit hallway, he paused and mock-saluted.

How was Aloysius to find three times the amount of the quarterly rents in under two months? What he wouldn't give to never have married Isobel, never to have purchased the vain acres outside Crookston, not to have lost so much at the tables! What was the honorable thing to do now? He could sell the small property, that would fetch almost all the amount needed outright. But then how would he live with a wife? Everyone would know he was a wastrel, rather than a cunning fellow. That was not how he intended his father to see him at the end of his life.

Chapter 23

Rafferty

Lennán sat up in his bed, an enormous improvement over the last weeks, but feeling nothing like an accomplishment. His back curved, feeling all its fifty-nine years of life and three weeks of convalescence.

Will I ever heave a mallet again, stretch leather 'cross a last, grasp a load of wood with confidence?

The bumpy, plain wall held no answers, but he knew them. He sat up and he closed his eyes, but the regret still came so forcefully up to his throat that he felt tears threaten. First it had been putting his two younger brothers into such danger that they needed to leave Ireland. Then it had been his failure to find work fast enough that had made them split up. He knew Feargal had been tossed on a boat to the penal colonies, naught to be done, but Murchadh had only gone as far as Liverpool for work, and still he'd lost him.

Those were his brothers. But his children! When Orla had gone to work at the manse, Lennán had not been able to argue with the child's logic. Before his wife had died, they had both wanted their oldest girl to be convent educated, but there were none nearby. So he figured she would have safe employment at the manse. But then to have his wee girl, grown up and whisked away by some pale tumphy of an Englishman!

He'd railed against her for leaving them, deserting him, casting aside her faith.

"But it will be one less mouth to feed, Father," she'd said meekly, that morning so long ago.

Now, so many years later, for her to come back, to reach out and be able to touch her—it was almost more than he could bear. He still tasted failure in his relationship with Orla. He wished he'd been a better man after his wife had died. Remorse and self-reproach were wedged in his soul along with the love.

She'd come back twice since his illness, he knew. His memory of the doctor's saving of him was practically nil, but his young wife told him it were Orla's doing: much as she begrudged giving the credit, she was honest. They had only talked once; the other time he must have been asleep. So much he had to say to her, but the lump in his throat prevented him. And she sat there waiting, attending him but not divulging too much of herself.

Lennán had little money to spare, and too many to divide it among, since he'd had to retire from the bleachfields from illness. But he wanted to make some sort of provision for his children.

Again, he wondered about his brothers, but gave up and spoke the prayer in his mind that God look after them better than he had.

Elspeth's tread sounded on the stairs, her clogs giving a dull thump set off by the slap of her hand on the railing. *I fashioned that railing. I could rally and do it again.*

"Len? Are you hungry, man?"

She stopped mid-stair so that only her head was above floor height. She could see him, but he could only see her flyaway hair and anxious eyes.

"Could do with a bite," he replied, knowing it was the answer that would suit her best. He saw her forehead immediately relax.

"Bring it up, or ye comin' down?" Elspeth's terseness, along with her honesty, were famous in the house, and even in the neighborhood. It had suited him when the children were talkative but during his convalescence it had felt so silent and tomb-like, he'd made a vow to speak up more.

"I might just try it," he said. "Maybe just a hand…" She was already by his side, crouching over to help hoist his larger frame out of the low cot. He almost lost his balance and crashed into the wall, but then they steadied, and she helped him down slowly. The rail helped too. Lennán willed strength into his back. He wanted it to be there next time his daughter came to call.

Chapter 24

O'Brien

The life of a journalist, O'Brien thought bitterly. Of all the possibilities he'd once tendered, this choice had not turned out as he'd thought it would. True, he'd risen higher than his place of birth would have forecast: a manure-filled barn right spang in the middle of Ireland didn't foretell much. But his mother had given him ambition, and the priests had fed it. *Damnation.*

He'd twice had to intercede for the sprightly Widow Smith, but he really couldn't do so again without committing himself, and he'd sworn not to get entangled. It would only twist up his ambitions into a thick hedge of knots, when what he wished to encourage was a strong, straight trunk, reaching up to the sky like the oak, ash, and yew in the forests he'd grown up near.

No, what he needed now was the ear of a banker or someone with charity for the cause and lots of money. The lectures he organized were always free and barely collected pennies, but at least the speakers waived their usual fees. Next week he had a doctor coming who had a very attractive theory about disease communication. He was trying to get taken on by a University. O'Brien knew well the curse of knowing of a great good, and being unable to connect it to the people who needed it. This Mr. Snow of Durham should have his work in several of his friends' papers, in the *London* papers.

No, he had neither the time nor the funds to go around protecting some fool woman without anyone to look after her. But—

Ever since he had seen her at that meeting, it was as if some song erupted from her skin that only he could hear. He'd looked away immediately, but her presence was like a source of heat: he could tell where she was without needing to look. That day at the shop, he had been following her on errands when he saw the self-important man jerk to a stop on the pavement and knew there'd be a commotion. Thank goodness he'd been there! What would she have done—!

She didn't give the impression of being frail, just incredibly inexperienced. She'd lived in Glasgow before, so he didn't know how she'd preserved such an air of naivety, other than that her goodness was simply untouched by the grime that surrounded them.

There had been that stripped-down moment when she had asked about his 'first desire in life' and deduced his motives. Did James dare ask if she shared the same desire at heart? It was in his throat to ask several times when they met at McNary's bookshop, but he kept up the cool facade. Too soon he would have to travel again, and the 'open schedule' lie would be apparent. He was always having to move through the country: the northern industrial cities, the western ports, the great slithering pile of London itself. He couldn't ask her to leave her hard-won comfort for that.

Back to writing, he told himself sternly. He flipped through the pages of his notebook til he found the notes for the next article: the doctor's speech. He took a sip of the strong coffee on offer at his favorite coffeehouse. Looking around, he saw none of his cohort, for which he was grateful. The coffeehouse was where he went for solitude, not bonhomie. Here, no one asked about his views, merely if he wanted another cup or more sugar. Here, no one saw through to the burning core of his being.

"Damn it all!" he burst out. The few other patrons looked up, alarmed.

James scooped up his notebook and pen tools with pique. He crammed them into his coat before pulling his arms through the sleeves and hurrying out of the shop. He might as well drink the coffee at McNary's if he was going to think about *her* all day.

Chapter 25

Orla

She had never meant to become involved.

Somehow it was December, and not only was she on the Petition Committee, but Mr. McNary had scheduled meetings with their coterie of journalists adjacent to the library's opening times so she could more easily attend. So now Orla listened in on plans for petitions, responses to editorials, and more. She was even beginning to form an idea of what went on in the bustling metropolis down south—at least as far as the political bargaining went.

Thankfully her diversification gamble had paid off so far, and while the first three months she had reinvested the dividends into the stock shares, she was now siphoning off a small percentage to go toward paying the fines of the still-defiant Unstamped Press. One of their number in London was in fact undergoing trial for not paying his stamp duties, but they hoped for a favorable result that acknowledged the injustice of the levy.

Today's Committee meeting involved a guest: a short, well-dressed man from London. His name was Levinson and Orla was leery of the glee that was trying to leap from his person. After he'd been introduced, she found out why.

"...And so, the Company will now be forced to negotiate a contract with each rajah and nabob on every import."

One of the journalists let out a low whistle. Another shushed him.

"Meaning...?" Bludkin prompted the speaker.

"Meaning a slight contraction of the Company's power. One that needs to be followed up with more demands! The Crown must know, Parliament must know, the carnage can not be allowed to continue!"

Orla frowned, feeling at a loss as to how this Crown policy in a faraway colony would affect their home interests. But then, the collapse of the fine cotton imports was the lead that had given her a way back to independence that summer, which restarted her hopes of a comfortable prosperity. But she needed to understand how it would play out with the players on the scene.

"Who will benefit?" she murmured to McNary, by whose side she always chose to sit. "Will the individual captains of ships be able to trade before the Company's? That doesn't seem right."

"I think the gentleman from London is mistaken," McNary murmured back. "This isn't a curb, it's setting the stage for the railway contracts."

"Ahh," she said, and settled back in her seat. The railways. Like the canals, there was a fever of speculation about the new infrastructure, and Orla couldn't stay far enough away from it. Even in India...her mind boggled.

There was some discussion of the consequences after he finished speaking, but generally, the men thought it too early to expend much effort; more evidence was needed. Once he had gone out, the regular journalists listened to one of their own divulge more immediately influential knowledge.

"The cotton spinners to the south, they're thinking seriously of a strike action."

It was McLean who spoke, the one among them who covered the textile mills to the southeast. He himself was from the Isles, and Orla wondered how he liked the city life if he'd grown up by the open sea.

"Without a sympathetic manager, the men at the Cumbernauld mill are agitating the most, though there are plenty at the surrounding establishments who are in talks about it too."

"Have they no thought of the danger of arrest?" another man asked, his voice shaken by frustration. The spinners were professional men, skilled and, at an earlier time, able to command a good wage for their families. Since the war, though, they'd suffered humiliating defeats due to the owners adopting sidelong tactics, and them not allowed to negotiate. Orla knew at least two of the men in the room had siblings who worked in those mills, though she didn't know if it was Cumbernauld or one of the others.

"Most certainly. They also have a mind to spies; they are careful."

Orla didn't have to look to know O'Brien was looking at her. She had not thought of the danger herself. Stupid, reckless.

"Are there any levers of power to be exerted on the recalcitrant owner? An MP? A Justice of the Peace? A family member, for god's sake." Another journalist, one of the few with silvery hair, shook his head regretfully.

They talked about possibilities to obviate such a strike, for in the present circumstances they knew it would be a disaster. Until the results of the stamp duty trial were known, they could not commit funds to a fellow cause, but perhaps after next week. *So many competing causes*, Orla fretted. *So many needs unmet.*

There was a lull in the commentary before they took the final motion to disband. Orla drew herself up.

"Has this group ever partnered with another group in matters of charity?"

An unexpected hush doused the table.

"I know your aims are to equip and motivate others to defend themselves, but in the matter of the strike, can we not call on others to supplement?"

"Whom would you suggest, Mrs. Smith?" asked the silvery-haired fellow.

"Well…I had reached out to the women of the Anti-Slavery Society for help in passing petitions. They were a little reticent to do so, but I think they would gladly help deliver food and medicines to families of those working at the mill, while the other levers of influence are pursued."

She swallowed. She was glad the thought had come to her at the last moment. She was relieved she could speak rationally, in front of all these learned men.

The idea was agreed to, and she was deputized to put forth the call and coordinate the effort. Atkinson handed her his card, and she was invited to call on his family on the Saturday. Graciously, she accepted the whirlwind. Calmly, she affirmed to herself that involvement in such things was the right thing to do. Her parents would have been proud of her, if they'd known.

Chapter 26

The wet season did not deter their charity-minded allies. The Anti-Slavery Society women were indeed more amenable to delivering food baskets, but their usual organizer was laid up with chilblains and couldn't be counted on to march round at speed. They made arrangements for another sister organization to send a sister of charity from a convent to dedicate to this neighborhood in particular, as Mr. Atkinson had pleaded their case so persuasively.

Orla learned this at the next meeting, in January. Everyone wished one another a happy 1834, with tales of children's delight and puddings saved and whiskies savored. Orla kept her composure amongst the jocularity. Her Christmas holiday had passed without much fanfare. She'd sent greetings to Mrs. Burch and Mrs. Darcy, to Mrs. Tate and Mrs. Grant. When she probed Mr. McNary, she learned he was not married, and so, no card for him.

She'd been invited for Christmas supper to her brother's and had the most extraordinary divided experience: part of her smiled and laughed and joined in the fun that the children's good humor produced, while the other part felt the crumbling away of a crater in her chest. *Why were we not blessed? Is this*

God's punishment? Should I go to the priest after so long? Have I a hope of remarrying?

It was a relief to send the children to bed and share a quiet spiced wine with Christopher and Serena before turning in, her usual room void of whispers or plans with no guests at the tavern. She'd returned to distribute her gifts for Boxing Day in Crookston and felt a little buoyed up by her small village friendships bearing the fruit of human kindness. But coming back here today to listen to the news rather swallowed it up again, for there was yet another group unable to make ends meet with their wages and hours as they were: coal miners with the new steam-pump. It kept them working underground for twelve hours and the reputation was good enough that it attracted plenty of men. So the mine owners felt no compunction in lowering the wage and seeing who would keep working.

"The women are falling down from exhaustion having to do everything, since the man's wage goes to the company store. They cook and clean, grow and preserve, just like a farmer's wife, without the farmer," said a square-jawed, intense-looking man at the table.

Orla hoped the new sister of charity would be enough to go round with the various districts that were living in human want. When she was young, there had been wretched suppers but there had always been extra work to supplement, and bodies to do it. Now it seemed the work was infinite but wages were stagnating, with children dying for lack of food.

She stayed briefly after to browse the new books brought in and sign out one volume of *Illustrations of Political Economy*. With a mild shock, she saw it was written by a woman. While she was rearranging the items around the large book in her satchel, O'Brien separated from the group to stand by her.

"Blessings of the New Year," he said, then cleared his throat. "Did you enjoy a good Christmas?"

She eyed him, wondering whether he would launch another campaign upon her right then. It seemed to be his way.

"Thank you, yes. I spent it with my family in Rutherglen." O'Brien knew about her brother there, of course, from explaining how events had transpired, but had never met them. "And you?"

"With some cousins in London." At her raised eyebrow, he added, "the stages are getting ever so much faster these days. Still a wild few nights, but they have the system down pat, it must be said."

She didn't know what to say to that. Surely he didn't hurry back for *her* sake.

"Are you following Mr. Sinclair's new series of lectures? They should be quite interesting."

"I'm not sure I recall the subject of Sinclair's offerings, no."

"He's publicizing the content of a new book by Mr. Sturge, who went to the colonies—the West Indies, of course—to document the situation among the slaves and explain how abolition and a free society might be obtained for the betterment of all involved. I daresay, Mrs. Smith, you have not heard much about the colonial plantation system?"

Other than as a mysterious place where young rich men went to die of disease or make their fortune?

"No," she answered.

"Then you'll allow me to escort you to the first assembly? Tis Tuesday next, in the hall by the Tron Church."

"In the evening?"

"Just so."

Orla paused, motionless as she considered what he was asking. He would escort her. She felt like a field mouse, frozen under the gaze of some hawk or harrier. Should she allow an escort? Or would that compromise all her newly won independence?

"Is this subject still on the same road to your Irish freedom?"

"I believe it is," he replied.

Does he consider me as an equal, a compatriot? Or an adornment, a tool? He met her gaze levelly, sanguinely. She let go of her breath and smiled slightly.

"Very well. I am interested."

He bowed and they followed the last of the party from the building to various carriages sent to collect them.

When Orla presented herself at the same building the following Tuesday, O'Brien was nearly late. He jumped from a hansom and held the door open to her startled eyes.

"Are you that busy these days, Mr. O'Brien?"

"Busy enough," he said, and she let the subject drop as the cabbie sped them away to the heart of the Merchant City.

Mr. Sinclair was a slight, preacherly-looking man. O'Brien pointed him out and she observed him greeting some members of his acquaintance. She leaned slightly in to her companion.

"Isn't it a harsh climate in the West Indies? He looks barely strong enough to withstand it."

"He is the publisher, not the author, recall."

"Ah, yes. Have you read his book already?" she asked.

"But of course." O'Brien winked at her, and pulled the volume from a pocket in his coat. *Narrative of Events since the First of August*, it read. "You may borrow my copy if you like, after you hear the accompanying speech. His publisher does the work proud. I was quite convinced."

And as Orla had learned, O'Brien was right in his estimation of a good speaker. Probably because he knew how to play the heart-strings himself. This man Sinclair explained the abuse of the islands, made them share his incomprehension at the brutishness of the regime that survived by the whip, not by authority or logic, and convinced them that it was not God's plan, nor a credit to the King, that it continue.

"The economics are disheartening. It is all Britain's coffers emptying to hold back the tide so that a few rich men may go out and pick up the gold left by the waves. I say let the tide go free and sweep them away, so that the earth may be washed clean!"

The room erupted in supportive calls and applause around them. O'Brien joined in and Orla did the same, yet not feeling the same swell that affected the others. Sure, the abolition bill had been pushed through last year by the skin of its teeth, thanks to the new Reform Members. But she'd always thought of the colonies as benefiting the rich while also giving a ladder to some of the men who went out as clerks and officers and returned richer, with expanded hopes for their children's futures. That wasn't even being mentioned here. She'd talk about it with O'Brien later.

However, he had to hurry off again afterward, and she found her steps directing themselves back to McNary's premises. When she entered and saw the silhouette at the desk, she smiled and browsed her way through to the back.

"Ah, Mrs. Smith. How lovely to see you. You are well, I trust?"

"Very well, thank you. And you, sir?"

"Very well. Have you read the editorial in the *Workingman*?"

"In Monday's? Yes, it was, ah, the one about the restrictions on issuing banks?"

"That's the one. I wrote it."

"Ah! Well done. Now I can tell you I only half understood it so you can explain it a bit more." She grinned and he sighed in mock exasperation: he was purely delighted.

"You know our banking system is different from England's." He raised an eyebrow in question.

"Yes, to our benefit, I believe." He waggled his head as if in debate.

"Perhaps. It is at least more cash-focused, depending as it does on local networks of trust since the Treasury is far away. You know the Ship Bank and British Linen?" Again he looked up for her confirmation before continuing. "Most banks started when a business had a need to carry custom over from year to year or ship to ship with its clients and suppliers. Now they're becoming much more sophisticated and talking of shares and discounts and—"

"Speculation." He didn't look up but pursed his lips.

"Some would indeed call it that. Others would call it lending at a higher rate to compensate for a higher risk."

"And that is what the Jews have typically done?"

"The riskier investments? Well, I believe they have been lending at all points since they were forced to stick to the few trades open to them. Lending, tailoring, goldsmithing. It is a queer mix." He screwed his face up in thought before abandoning this line of thought. "But the restrictions—the Treasury is issuing new rules about who can issue bills and how much they must have on hand to back them up. This makes trouble for our businesses in Scotland, as well as our branches here in Glasgow. Especially because of the enormous money that will be flowing to the slavery repayment debt."

"Oh yes, that was mentioned—they are still looking for the bankers powerful enough to pull it off, you said in the editorial? I shouldn't wonder. Twenty million pounds...I cannot even conceive of it."

"I fear many of the small banks will be crushed under the pressure of the new rules and the loss of custom as the gold flies to the big lenders or the Government." McNary sighed. "It is an uncertain field. And still not a robust climate."

"You fear another bust?" Orla narrowed her eyes, her thoughts paging through all her points of vulnerability if he was right.

"Many of us do. But there's no sure way to weather it. Gold? Land? Cash paper? That is the least likely of all, though the others are uncertain. I'm afraid it is power that will dictate safety, as usual." He looked at her, sadness dimming his wry smile.

Chapter 27

Two more months passed, accustoming Orla to the habit of anticipating her monthly reports from her shares and stocks, calculating how much could be reinvested, and apportioning another percentage to the strike fund of the journalists. McNary had just presented her with the idea that she, as a good broker, be their banker, and she was considering it.

The sister of mercy sent from one of the northern towns had been doing a fairly good job of organizing the food distribution in the mining districts to the east. She'd met with her once, a Sister St. Clarence, and was due to meet with her again today about future monies for the strike fund. Orla vehemently wished for something more permanent, less dependent on charity, to be the succor of these stubbornly independent people, but nothing had materialized.

Life in Crookston was much the same. Her circle took little notice of the bills Parliament passed, or the new politicians that sometimes appeared at the train station being built south of the river. The butcher still took her mail, the sisters Arbischer still dropped in, mostly unannounced. The only glaring omission from the previous year was Isobel. She'd decamped to join her earl's son so fast that there had been no leave-taking, a fact that had scandalized the small community. Orla had heard from the dairy farmer's family that lived close by that she'd even left furniture, presumably because her new husband had not thought it fine enough to bother with sending a conveyance for.

Orla had no love for Tate but she hoped Isobel was happy in her new marriage. She planned to travel to her old friends once again, and contented herself with the knowledge that true friends could still be found, even if it was at the other end of the island.

The small details that changed with the season and with Orla's once-again-assured nest egg were noticeable to those who looked, however. When she returned from Glasgow, a hamper was delivered with delicacies that couldn't be procured in the village. And after the splurge on the new half-mourning dresses the previous spring, they were followed by plans for three new bright and fashionable dresses this year. The cloth had been chosen at the warehouse, the modiste was in Town, but the villagers knew, somehow.

This chilly day, Orla wrapped up warmly to visit her brother and father and stay over once again at the inn. Storms were predicted so it would be a slow week for custom, according to Christopher, so they'd planned for a full table, their father's family coming over to the tavern and joining them for a full celebration of Candlemas. She only had that meeting with Sister St. Clarence in the afternoon to worry about before heading over.

They'd agreed to meet outside Tron Church. The sister then invited Orla behind the church to where the priests lived and served them each a cup of tea and a biscuit.

"Thank you for the cup. It is quite dreary out."

"Oh, aye. Not a great day for traveling about. I hope you're pleased with the progress, Mrs. Smith?"

"Right to business! Indeed. You've done a very fair job of things, Sister. I only wish we didn't have to be going on so. The men in the district work so hard, they should be able to buy the things they need, not depend on charity to keep body and soul together."

"I know it. You said they would try to pressure the bad owner into changing his mind. No luck with that?"

"Not that I've heard. Not a religious man, unfortunately, or I'd turn you to that task as well." Orla smiled at her. The woman, quite a few years younger, perhaps, smiled back, and something in the softening expression rang alarm bells in her chest. Why did it feel so familiar?

"You came from Manchester, isn't that right?"

"That's where I've lived most of my majority, yes. But I grew up proper in Liverpool. You, ma'am?"

"I? I, uh, here, actually. Here in Glasgow, though I've traveled a fair bit since coming back. And you—would you mind if I asked your family name?"

"No, it's Rafferty, ma'am. My father—ma'am?"

Orla's hands had flown to her face, covering her nose and mouth, shocked beyond speech. She heard her father's voice telling about his brothers when she was a child. Once even about the failed rebellion that had sent them all scattered across the sea. She knew she had family she'd never seen: one brother to Liverpool, one brother to Australia, or so her father had assumed. He'd never written to them or searched them out, considering himself as the oldest to be the one they would come back to. But they never had, in over thirty years.

"Who—who's your father?" she asked, though she knew it already.

"Murchadh Rafferty, why—are you—are you family?" And now this woman, all brisk and business-like, had eyes that glimmered like hers.

"My father is Lennán Rafferty. Our fathers are brothers. Is he —alive?"

"Yes," the woman gulped, nodded, swallowed. "Good Lord."

Orla laughed. "Good Lord, indeed! I'm Orla, the oldest. I have a brother, Christopher, who lives nearby too. Would you like to meet them?"

"I—" She gave in to the same embarrassed laughter Orla had. "Goodness. I didn't much think of the possibility when I answered the call from the Society. But to be delivered right to you!"

She reached out a hand and Orla took it.

"My name's Amelia, and I'm the youngest—or, that is, the youngest of his first wife."

"My father's remarried as well." They paused a moment, acknowledging in silence their mothers' deaths. Orla didn't want to explain about her estrangement with her father because of her marriage. Didn't want to introduce the strangeness of her conversion into this soft space.

"Goodness." Orla let go her hand to sip her tea, which had gone cool. "Amelia."

Her cousin looked up, and Orla saw the plump Irish cheeks and deep-set eyes. Soft skin. And something compelled her to admit the thing she didn't want to.

"I'm going to visit my father and brother tonight. We haven't all been together in years. A result of my marriage and moving away, and…no longer going to Mass."

Her cousin looked down, adjusting her preconceptions without showing her eyes, Orla noticed. A family tendency.

"But I am a widow nigh on two years. We are in the same town now and working to patch things up. I should be delighted to introduce you to more family tonight, if you've no prior obligations. I'm sure they'll be astonished and delighted to hear about your family. As am I."

When Sister St. Clarence finally looked up again, she didn't speak, but nodded hurriedly. They held hands again, and talked quietly for some time before leaving the vestry.

Chapter 28

The families were completely bowled over. Orla and Amelia—Sister St. Clarence—had decided to introduce her as her religious name first to see if anyone could see the family connection before revealing her family name. No one had, and the gasps and claps when the truth was revealed had them in tears all over again.

Amelia was tasked with recounting her growing up, and Orla's father paid particular attention.

"It's like I said to Orla; we grew up in Liverpool, leastways til I was about seven years old. Then Da moved us to Manchester for a better job. Our mother was a cleaner and could find a job easy when we were younger. Anyway, we were there just in time for Da to get caught up in the radical politics of the day. You know what happened in '19."

Lennán's young children looked to their father. Christopher's looked to their mother. Amelia waited, but as neither parent stepped into the gap, she continued with her narrative.

"Peterloo. A great crowd of people listening to speeches, and the soldiers called out ended by killing innocent bystanders in the crowd. A massacre, they call it now. It was—a scary turn for my father. He—he fled to America."

"He what!" exclaimed Lennán. A glow lit up his blue eyes, but whether it was pain or anger or something else entirely, Orla could not guess.

"He's still there," Amelia admitted. "He's written us once a year for thirteen years. He wrote to Eilis as the oldest, and she wrote back of course, but…only when she told him mum had met her reward did his next letter contain the news of his… other family."

The sharp hiss around the room—Christopher's wife's, Lennán's wife, Lennán himself—was sanction enough. Amelia bowed her head. Orla groped for her hand.

"I'm sorry, cousin." Perhaps Orla's admission of her estrangement had made it easier for Amelia to reveal this. Amelia patted her hand. Nodded.

"It took us some time, some conversations among us, some visits to the priest. We decided to let it go by the way. He hadn't meant harm, he'd been governed by fear, and he'd tried to spare her feelings. But it was…hard."

Orla wasn't sure this recitation was suitable for the young children, but they looked solemnly on.

"I've found my path as a nun, and even in this country it suits me well. Though someday perhaps I'll ask to be sent back. When the time feels right."

"So Murchadh is in America all this time." Her father spoke slowly. "At least I couldn't have found him if I'd tried…but I do wish I'd tried when he was…" He turned his attention to Amelia again. "Could I have his address, my colleen?"

"Of course, Uncle. Shall I write it down for you now?" A scrap of paper was fetched so she could copy it over for him.

"Pennsylvania," he sounded out. "Sounds like a forested place. Is he…happy there, then? What's his occupation?"

"I've never been, but his letters do make him sound well and happy, Uncle. He makes his way as a machinist, making tools."

There was a pause in the conversation, as Lennán sought to hide his feelings again after his display. Everyone else busied themselves finishing up every last bit of sauce with their heel of bread or potato and finally the cutlery and crockery sounds were finished also.

With a sigh of satisfaction, Lennán turned to his new niece. "A warm welcome to ye. We are glad Orla found ye by chance. Providence has mercy on us."

"Amen" echoed several times.

Orla thought about her uncle at a forge in Pennsylvania the rest of the night.

Chapter 29

Still sorting out her astonishment at the discovery of a branch of her family, Orla went about her tasks on Saturday slowly. The cat was happy to be indoors by her fire. And she was happy to be snug at home with a cup of tea while the wind lashed outside.

Why had her uncle Murchadh never written to his brother? Was he also estranged from the third brother in the Antipodes? Was Amelia really a believer, or had the convent simply been the only place to take her in? What of Amelia's other siblings—where were they? Would her father write to his brother in America?

She had wanted to grill the woman along with everyone else last night but she saw that her father had thought only of his young brother. She hadn't wanted to cause him more grief, so they shelved the revelations for another time. Orla was staying with the Catholic schoolteacher in a neighborhood by Rutherglen, and had promised to come again the next week. *It looks like I was the gradual thaw, and cousin Amelia is starting the flames.* Orla grinned. She was glad to be back in a rhythm with her family again, and hoped past decisions would no longer poison the air between them.

She considered her social engagements. This evening she would be hosting the sisters for supper, and Tuesday morning was her library visit. Almost a year she had been going now, she thought with a jolt. She followed most news quite easily now, after repeated questions put to the patient McNary. She'd met with all her chosen firms twice now, and while there remained some markets—and people—to watch, she didn't see anything near as crooked as what had happened with Oswald. She hoped they got their reprimand and fall from grace and learned from it. Could she breathe a sigh of relief at the near-miss? She had a feeling something from her misadventure was still hanging over the affair, waiting to fall.

She clucked at her paranoia and got up to refill the kettle and pet Levern.

"They'll be their own downfall, won't they, Lev? Didn't need me to sit on the scale. That fool solicitor and that dratted peacock at the sweet shop… men and their tempers. I'm glad you haven't got one."

She sorted through correspondence and replied to a few missives. She started chopping vegetables from the cold shed for her dinner. When they were simmering in a broth fragrant with herbs over the fire, she sat back down. She reached for the last book she'd borrowed, the one from O'Brien about the conditions on the West Indian plantations. She'd been putting off starting it since the lecture, taken up thinking about Amelia —Sister St. Clarence—but it seemed a good time to start.

Two hours later, the smell of bitterness tore her away from the page.

"The soup!" She jumped up to peer in and saw that her broth had disappeared, the vegetables boiled down to a sticky mass at the bottom of the tin pot. "Agh!"

She hurried for a dipper of water and heard it sizzle as she poured. At least the fire was low. She prodded at the vegetables and saw that they hadn't turned to charcoal quite yet. A sigh of relief. More water. More bacon fat. She glanced at the clock and gasped.

"No wonder!"

Once the soup was saved, her thoughts turned back to the horrors of the world she'd been reading about. There was little theory or logic involved in the book. It read like a diary of horrors, consisting of categories of harm, rates of death, types of weapons used—Orla felt as if all the blood had left the upper half of her body. She felt quite cold. Putting a back of a hand to her cheek, she realized it was her hands that had gone so cold.

She stoked the fire, briefly considering adding more potatoes to the soup but discarded the idea. She shredded in the kale and let it go soft before fishing it all out and setting out cutlery for their modest meal.

Just then, the knock sounded on the door. Remembering to be careful, she didn't call out as she used to, but opened the door a smidge to see.

"Louise, Betsy! Come in and welcome."

She saw Louise wrinkle her nose at the still-present acrid smell.

"Should be ready in just a minute. Go on and dry your cloaks."

They unburdened themselves and hung their coats on the hall tree. Orla had placed a couple cloths directly under the hooks to catch any drops and protect the floor. Betsy noticed.

"Ah, clever job, that!"

Orla just looked and nodded. She was putting out the bread board and serviettes.

"Lucky you, staying in all day," Betsy said.

"Is it very bad out?"

"That wind is fearful chill!" answered Louise. "It's a good day to stay in, I'd say."

Orla sighed. "I've got appointments next week, so I hope it calms down before then. Anyway, how are you both?"

They chatted as the food was served out and said a short grace before chatting some more, amiably and familiarly, the way Orla wished she had been able to do with her family for so long. She glanced at her friends, seeing past the widow and the spinster to their worrying and cherishing hearts.

"You still keeping up with those newspapers of yours?" Betsy asked. "I know you take several in a week."

"Boggles my mind," Louise said with a teasing smile.

"Yes…" Orla was distracted as she thought of reading. She hadn't seen these ladies since the revelation of her cousin, and she wanted to relay the news, but her reading…if she brought it up, would they recoil? She realized she didn't talk politics with the sisters, only personal issues.

"It isn't bad news, is it?" Betsy set down her spoon to touch Orla's arm in comfort.

"No, not…there is news, but it's not what is on my mind today. I…I've been reading Mr. Sturge's visit to the West Indies. It's…awful."

"Oh," pronounced Louise. "Who's he?"

Her sister spoke, voice softened. "He's an abolitionist. They say he has a book coming out that is going to paint the West India lobby in a bad light. Is it true? Is it in the papers?"

"I have the book—pamphlet, really. It's truly horrible."

Betsy looked to her sister then back at Orla. "But it's not something that affects *you*, right? You've nothing to do with the sugar barons. That's Mrs. Foxton—I mean, Mrs. Tate's affair now."

"Just because one is not profiting from something doesn't make it less awful," Louise commented.

"I agree, Mrs. Lockhaven. I very much agree." Louise looked at her sister as if she was at a loss to explain. Orla was not up to trying. "I have also had some good news," she said, easing them away from the horrors. They looked up expectantly.

"As part of the strike funds, we appealed to the Anti-Slavery Society in Manchester to send us someone to help minister to the working families while the negotiations were ongoing. They are not on strike, but they are still half-starving," she explained. Betsy surprised her by speaking.

"Is that not something a lady here might do? Why'd ye have to send to Manchester? Seems a long way."

"It is, but the journalists who are on the committee did not know any of the local organizations, and the sister convent in the neighborhood is already stretched thin with poor aid. Anyway, the woman they sent turned out to be a cousin I've never met."

Both their jaws dropped.

"Cousin!"

"How?"

Orla smiled. "My father came here with his two brothers. One was sent to Australia," she said, ducking her head, "for some paltry crime, while the other went to find work in Liverpool. He never heard from either of them again."

"But that's extraordinary!"

"And they're still alive, both of them?"

"Why did he never write? It's only Liverpool."

Orla considered. "I'm not sure if Father's youngest brother knew how to write...and I think on all sides, there's been a feeling of shame about the family being cast apart. I know I haven't been on the best of terms with my father, but we're trying to mend things now. He's very...regretful."

"And has he met this cousin?"

"Yes—I brought her along to our supper last night, at Christopher's inn. A bigger surprise I couldn't have even devised!" Brief laughter. "But the shock was followed by a warm welcome, so all's well. I'm eager to spend more time with her. Amelia, her name is, though she goes by Sister St. Clarence."

"A nun," Betsy was shaking her head and clucking her tongue. "Your poor family."

Orla sat up a little straighter. The sisters didn't always come across the way they meant to.

"She only means that—" Louise began.

"I only meant that she must have been driven by great need to sacrifice so much," Betsy said hurriedly. "I had no idea you had Catholics in the family."

"Yes," Orla said simply.

"But you're not one, are you?" Louise asked.

Orla paused, realizing it was the first time she'd been asked this for a long time. She'd thought of it many a time in her head, of course, but saying it out loud crystallized things so.

"No," she finally said. "Though I was baptized and confirmed as one. I left it behind for my marriage."

The silence settled on the trio. Betsy digested her reasoning while Louise looked thoughtful.

"Is your father wanting you to return to the fold, then?"

"You've a keen eye, Louise. I'm not sure. He hasn't spoken of it, but…I'm glad for the upheaval of the cousin." She gave them a wry smile. "Heaven knows what I'll do until Uncle Fergal reappears!"

Chapter 30

Orla sometimes wondered if she shouldn't get her own carriage. She did so many errands these days that living out in Crookston made for a lot of hired hacks and the miserable weather made them hike up the fare. But when she calculated the salary of a coachman, a groom, the keep of a horse, the carriage itself…she settled back into the squabs of the hansom, folding the edges of her cloak over her hands for added warmth.

She hurried to find a hansom home after her final fitting for her new dresses. A dark green, a blush pink, and a brown-and-white stripe: only a few minor changes still to complete. The sleeves on the coat, however, had needed a lot more havering over. But she'd be grateful when she had it on later that month. As she was figuring which day it would be ready, a shadow in front of her caught her attention. The light from a tavern was behind her, so someone was—

Just as she turned she had the impression of something swinging down upon her—and ducked. Something connected with the back of her neck and she cried out. She stumbled, reaching out for the ground. She regained her balance on all fours and a second later the pain from her spine made her cry out again. She tried not to move but look around with her eyes, scared of an unseen assailant coming to finish her off.

But as she crouched, trembling, and waited for a sound, she heard scuffling that appeared to be moving away. She risked moving to stand and whimpered at the pain arrowing down her arms. Rather than do more, she stood with a hand on the building she'd been walking beside and closed her eyes, breathing deep and then listening with all of her being.

Why now? Who was that? Was it chance? Or was it someone from that nasty group of shifty importers? One of them knew my face...

It was late on a Tuesday afternoon, and the street should have been busier, even with the early winter dusk but it was strangely silent. Orla couldn't hear the scuffling sounds anymore. She opened her eyes slowly.

A door creaked open, then another.

"Are you all right, miss?"

"What the devil!"

"Those ruffians again..."

The first query was uttered by a thickset woman with bright red hair. She hurried to Orla's side and took her hand. "Shall I help ye to a seat, missus?"

"I'm all right, it's—agh!" As she tried take a step and straighten, blinding pain shot down her spine again. "It hurts," she said, her eyes pouring out the proof, as involuntary as a brook.

"Tom!" the woman called. A large young man rushed to the door, saw his mother's raised hand, and ran over double-quick.

"Yes, ma'am?"

"This lady's had a blow to the back, and can't well walk. Carry her in, I'm going for the doctor."

"No, I'm—" She tried to forestall the fuss but another shriek was torn from her lips as the young man bent to pick her up and carry her inside. She could see nothing but white. She heard them but could no longer see anything. And that's when she truly began to fear.

She must have blacked out. She became aware of concerned, hushed voices, and a great many soft things pressed against her body, reclined on a sofa.

"Did ye see him, though? Was it 'im?"

"I didn't get a good look! Damn the man."

"Gerry! Language. She's waking up already."

Orla really didn't want to wake up to a crowd of interested well-wishing strangers, but there was nothing for it. She cautiously opened her eyes. The redheaded woman was there, the closest in her range of vision.

"How are you, pet? Can you see all right now?"

Orla blinked. She swallowed in order to speak and jerked at the pain in her neck the slight movement caused. A tortured groan escaped her lips at the same time she had to cough. There was simply too much going on at once in the same few inches.

The woman hovered over her, reaching for something, holding it to her lips.

"The doctor said to try not to move your neck, but you should drink some water. Have a wee swallow, just one, then rest, a'right?"

Orla bundled her courage enough to swallow through the pain, bore it, then lay there, panting. She licked her lips to speak.

"Thank you, Mrs. —?"

"I'm Mrs. Pilcher, my husband owns this tavern."

"And what time..."

"It's just past eleven o'clock."

The pain had abated. Orla considered. "You called a doctor? What did he say?"

"A nasty knock on the spine, but it'll just be a bruise, he wagers. Dreadful hard to move for a few days, but shouldn't be too long before you're up and about again." Orla sighed in relief as minutely as she could.

"Thank you, Mrs. Pilcher. Did anyone catch who it was?"

She looked up across the sofa but Orla caught herself before turning to look. A male voice this time. The hulking son who had carried her in?

"I tried to catch him, missus, but I've a lame foot. He was a tall, straight fellow, wearing a cocked hat and a full cloak. Soft boots, too, for they made little sound as he got away. Blast it."

"This is Mr. Pilcher, missus. Excuse his language."

Orla's eyes closed and she indulged in a bit of humor in her situation.

"Tis a pity you couldnae guddle the trout, master," she said in their own accent, that of the River Clyde's villages. After a split second of shock, it earned her a guffaw from the husband and a look of consternation from the wife.

"Dinna worry. I'm from here, but have had a long way coming back, that's all. If I can stay here til I can move—tomorrow morning? I can pay for the night. I live in Crookston now."

The confusion cleared and Mrs. Pilcher was solicitous again.

"Of course, missus."

"That's a good one, miss. I'm very sorry the blackguard caught you one. The doctor recommended cool compress, not hot, so we've got the bucket right here, change out when you need it." The man tapped on the side of a tub next to the sofa. Orla took it in at the edge of her vision.

"The rascal didn't even take your purse, my Tom was that hot on his tail, so there's that to be thankful for," added Mrs. Pilcher.

"Yes. Well. Thank you again," she said. "I shall see you in the morning?"

They nodded and withdrew from the room. It seemed like a first floor room, with how dry everything seemed, and Orla dreaded the walk down the stairs in the morning. She carefully lifted a hand to feel behind her head. The compress had warmed to her body temperature, so she gingerly tugged it free, dunked it in the bucket of cold water, and replaced it, with only a few involuntary grunts of pain. She was well swathed in blankets, and felt snug and warm other than being immobilized.

She closed her eyes again and tried to recall any details about the blow that might help her determine what had happened.

The fact that the man hadn't taken her purse certainly made it seem personal rather than a random crime. The face of that livid man from the sweet shop swam into her memory, but it wasn't a clear picture at this remove.

How was she to move tomorrow? Could she call on Betsy and Louise? How long would it take her to recover? She knew the doctor's opinion, but it had taken so long for her father's strength to return.

She focused on all the good things that had happened in the last year. Pictured each memory in her mind and drew them close like a quilt: a bulwark against her chilly prospects.

Chapter 31

In the event, the kind Mrs. Pilcher waited an extra hour after
their normal breakfast before knocking on the door to Orla's
room.

"Come in," she called faintly.

"Oh, my dear," the woman said, coming to her side. "Still too
bad, is it?"

"Yes," Orla said breathlessly. "I wonder if you could take a
note to a friend to ask her to come and help me home?"

"Yes, if you write—"

"That will be impossible, I'm afraid. Can you write?"

The woman cleared her throat and yelled for her son.

"Tom can. I wouldn't trust anyone to decipher my letters,"
she said sheepishly. When he arrived promptly, she sent him
after pen and ink. The note to the Arbischer cottage was
dictated and sent out for delivery.

"Thank you. Very much."

"That's all right. We'll leave you then until there's an answer.
I'll send Tom up with some more cold water and be in with a
broth in a wee while. Would you be wanting the chamber pot?"

At the very mention, Orla's bowels seized up in agony. She
struggled, imagining in a flash the indignity of being helped,

compared to the indignity of trying and falling and making a greater mess. "Yes, if I could pull me up…"

The task was accomplished with minimum fuss, Orla was grateful, and she could wait in peace without moving another muscle for the rest of the day if need be.

After another round of cold compresses and a half-bowl of broth, she slept a little, waking up to a clatter up the stairs.

"Mrs. Smith!"

"Oh, Mrs. Smith, how dreadful!"

"We've come to ferry you home—"

"Let's get you up, there—"

And once the awkward, painful rising was done, Orla was able to walk fairly normally; it was holding the head up as she reclined that was excruciating. She'd rarely been more glad of the pair of sisters than during that ride home—which was also excruciating, even though the road was soft and wet rather than dry and bumpy. She acknowledged their curiosity to distract herself on the journey home.

"It wasn't a blow to the head, Betsy. He missed—"

"Thank goodness!"

"But it wasnae an…insalubrious part of town, now was it? So why—"

"You mustn't go about so much on your own, Mrs. Smith—"

"He caught me on the top of the spine," Orla enunciated. "He likely meant to deal me a gash to the head and end me, but I ducked just in time."

Louise sucked in a breath. "The cad," she whispered.

"The doctor said bruising will be very painful for a few days, but not permanent. Honestly, it's the lying down and getting up that puts stars in my vision. It's fine. I shall sleep up against the wall."

Her friends groaned and she managed a weak smile.

"Are you afraid he'll follow you to your cottage?" asked Louise.

"We're taking you to our place, anyway," put in Betsy. "Otherwise, you'd have no chance."

"Thank you so very much for coming to rescue me." She looked at them both, one across and one beside. "And it is a good thought, about the cottage. Though," she paused. "If he knew where I lived, he wouldn't have had to accost me in the street. That seems harder to manage. I didn't know I'd be walking that way until…"

Her brain jumped to life and an idea kindled. Her words trailed off. She was aware of the sisters glancing at each other but kept her revelation to herself.

"Anyway, he didn't succeed, and we shall pray for his apprehension and swift conviction."

"Hear, hear!"

She settled in to an invalid's bed and a propped-up sleeping station for the next couple of days, leaning on the sisters more emotionally than they realized. Certainly Betsy was as enlivened from the additional social contact as Orla was bolstered by their company. When she left, she gave them each a gift, one that she'd had Jimmy run over to the butcher's to fetch.

She entered her cottage for the first time in three days to find it dusty and still. While she stood still in the doorway, she heard a cart behind. Turning abruptly, she winced. *S'all right, no need to jerk yourself around so, be easy now.*

The cart was laden with boxes round and square, packages large and little. Four of the larger ones came off once the driver had inspected the tags.

"Shall I set them inside, ma'am?"

"Right here, please," she said, indicating a spot inside the doorway. She didn't want him inside at all, but knew she shouldn't bend down to pick things up yet. He gave her a sidelong expression but complied.

"Could I trouble you to fetch some water for me as well?"

After he did so, she wished him well on his way, closed the door and leaned back on her clasped hands.

The thought that had come to her in the carriage: she'd been walking back from the modiste's. Before the fitting, she'd paid an account at the warehouse where she'd purchased her fabrics. The warehouse was along the river, near where the shipyards lay. And the neighborhood of the shipyards…was near to where Tate's family lands lay.

Could that so-called gentleman of oily grace be one of the colluders she'd overheard? She did not know who else had shares in Oswald's firm, but she knew she had not seen Isobel since her marriage to the man, at the time of her father's illness in August. Could it be someone else, unknown to her but similarly situated, who harbored ill feelings?

Orla was feeling a little faint and finally moved to dip a cup into the pail of water he'd left on the table. She drank, standing, and considered what to do.

She'd already leaned on the sisters far too much. Their purse would need to recover from the hansom fare and the extra victuals, for they would not let her repay them. She wanted to reach out to her new friends, but felt it might be unseemly: unmarried men at a widow's door? It had already caused half a scandal last autumn.

When she thought of seeking the advice of her family, she felt torn in two directions. She should be able to call on them but it still felt new, despite the regular meals and polite letter, despite the engaging presence of the ebullient Amelia. But she really did need help. Could she depend on those fragile threads? Should she ask it of them, growing families with their own worries?

Chapter 32

Christopher

The note read, "Dear Brother, Please come round for a visit this evening. I've need of your memory and experience. I've also asked Mr. O'Brien, as he has complementary knowledge to yours. Give my best to Serena and the children. Orla."

Olive had brought it in, and stood waiting to hear his answer.

"Is she coming? Aunt Smith?"

"No," he said shortly. Christopher was a little perturbed at the tone. "She's asked me to come to her."

"Well, why haven't we yet?"

"It is likely a small place, not big enough to accommodate us all, even if we had the leisure to leave the tavern unmanned."

"But you're going now." Olive's dark eyes implored. Christopher looked back at the letter. Caught between an ill feeling and a pleading look, he gave in.

"All right. Tell your mother we're off to Crookston for supper but to save us a piece." Olive flew to hug her father then ran to deliver the instructions. Christopher remembered he'd meant to go visit Orla about something disturbing several months ago, but events had intervened. They had a way of doing that in their busy courtyard.

O'Brien

O'Brien received a note at his habitual office, a pub on Argyle street:

"Dear Sir, Please come visit me at your earliest convenience. There is a matter of great importance to me that you may be able to render assistance on; it is of some urgency. I've also asked my brother to come, as I believe you both know useful information to be shared. Sincerely yours, Mrs. O. Smith."

James's brow furrowed. Her brother? What could they help each other with? He'd never met the man. He hurriedly finished his plate of brawn and potatoes and clapped his hat on his head before searching out a cab. A flutter in his belly recalled the memory of the incensed man outside the sweet shop; James had a bad feeling about this.

James, traveling less distance, arrived quickly. He walked from the crossroads, remembering to appear calm only when two persons observed his passing with interested eyes. He knocked on Mrs. Smith's door, and she was a bit slow in coming to open it. When she did, his hunched shoulders relaxed. She looked peaky, but collected.

"Ah, you've come! Good afternoon. Come in, Mr. O'Brien, please."

"Thank you. I was worried. You seem so reluctant to ask for help, that..."

"...that I must really be in trouble now, is that it?"

They sat down. She looked rather stiff, but he didn't assign much value to it. People their age were getting all sorts of aches and creaks.

"Tea?" She proffered, and he accepted. As she handed him the cup, he felt it time to ask.

"So what is it about?"

"I would prefer to tell the tale only once, so if you wouldn't mind, I shall wait for my brother to arrive. He shouldn't be too much longer."

Surprised, James assented.

"May I ask…is it to do with the man who came after you with that spy nonsense a few months ago?"

"I believe so. I also believe there may be someone else involved. I wouldn't like to give up my share in the campaigns, but if I continue to experience threats, I'm afraid I—" She gulped. "Well, I'm afraid."

James gave her what he hoped was a steadying look.

"Has something happened? Are you all right?" His voice was low. He reassessed her stiff movements. The flutter in his belly started to push up his throat.

"I'm quite all right now, Mr. O'Brien." She sipped her tea then motioned toward the door. "There, I believe that is Christopher. Would you get the door?"

Orla

The voice of her niece made Orla's eyes go as big as saucers. *What's she doing here? Did he misunderstand my message?* She wanted to put her face in her hands but knew it would still be a painful movement.

"Christopher! But…" She stood, pushing off the arm of her chair, to look at Olive. The girl was beaming at her, and looking thrilled to come on a visit, thrilled to see her. The girl's expression immediately altered when she saw how her aunt stood up.

"Aunt Smith! Are you hurt?"

Before her brother could even take his bearings in the cottage, Olive came over and leaned up toward her, still a foot shorter.

Orla tried to look down without moving her neck, but knew she must look like an angry headmistress keeping so ramrod-straight. She settled for taking her seat again, carefully.

"Olive! It's very nice to see you but it is a surprise. I asked for your father's help on a matter of business. I don't think—"

"Oh, but I wanted to come see where you live! I'll be quiet and listen. I just didn't want to miss the chance. The first time." The girl smiled uncertainly, probably wondering if she should press her former question. Orla sighed.

"Very well. You shall be a grown girl, listening to this conversation. Christopher, pull over the chair. There we are. Now," she said, looking at Olive, "this is in the strictest confidence, so no mentioning what I tell you outside these walls, you understand?" When her niece had nodded, and she met the gazes of the two men as well, she continued.

"Three days ago, I was walking along Govan Quay when I saw a shadow behind me—and ducked. I was hit by some ruffian, rather smartly, but thankfully he just caught me on the spine, not the head."

Both men had flinched when she said she'd been hit; Olive merely remained on the stool by her, eyes wide, mouth open.

"I was thoughtfully cared for by the owner of an inn nearby, Mrs. Pilcher, and helped home the next day by Mrs. Lockhaven and Miss Arbischer, friends here in the village. They are very good to me."

She cleared her throat here, feeling uncomfortable with the reference to the people she had gone to first, before the family and friends present.

"I didn't want to trouble anyone, but I am worried that this is related to my misadventures last year with the Oswald firm, and not some random street crime. Christopher, you remember I overheard a few of the meetings in your tavern and acted on that information—to my regret. And Mr. O'Brien, you remember I had to ask Mr. Grant for immediate assistance to remove my funds from London to Oswald's, then again to other, more above-board firms. That was why. I then had Mr. McNary send an anonymous letter to a newspaper about the base cheating that Oswald was resorting to and it created a bit of a stir."

"One that cleaned out his cash reserves," O'Brien agreed. "I believe one of the other journalists claimed it as his own discovery."

"Yes, well. I hope he does not have the same threats. Anyway, one of the men from the meeting recognized me some months later and accused me on the street. It would have been a greater scene if Mr. O'Brien hadn't been there to issue counter-threats, but as it was, I was made aware that there was bad feeling among the group I'd overheard, and it was directed at me."

Christopher, gawping most of this time, looked at his daughter in amazement.

"Orla, all this has been going on and you're only now telling me?"

"You were taking care of Father. I didn't think it would go any further."

Her brother blew out a frustrated breath and scrubbed his face with his hands.

"But three days ago, I was coming from Govan Quay." She paused. "And I wonder if our Mr. Tate, so recently married to my friend Isobel Foxton, might have made one of the group that were harmed by my letter."

"Tate...I do believe there was one of them on the list when we took wine orders."

"Who's this?" said O'Brien, looking lost.

"A gentleman who may be in need of funds," Orla said tightly. "He's a son of an earl, but a gambler, I believe. He's just been married, which will have cost him, and purchased a small country estate by Crookston, which will also have cost, and if he was mixed up with Oswald, he'll be in even worse hot water now."

"And he'd be able to connect you with that failure because..."

"Isobel knew about my going to the Fighting Tabby, that my brother owned it. She knew I was having financial difficulties. She—may have been the link," she finished.

A silence followed. Orla was about to break it by asking the men for proof when she felt a light touch on her sleeve.

"Aunt Smith? Have you a comfrey salve? If not, I saw some by the road as we came, I could—"

"Oh no—" Orla had shaken her head without thinking, jarring her vertebra again. "No," she said again, teeth gritted. "I'm fine for the moment, but thank you, Olive." She shot her brother an appreciative look but he was looking baffled.

"It is a good sounding theory, Orla, but how are we to prove it? Without any more danger to you? And then, how to stop them from threatening you like this? Or if it is not them?"

"Yes," O'Brien agreed. "I thought the threat of exposure would be enough. But perhaps this blasted Tate has told the whole circle. That would be very bad indeed."

"Bad enough to consider going to the police?" Christopher asked.

Orla and O'Brien shared a knowing glance. It was a complicated affair, and the police would not be able to see past the man accusing a woman; he would doubtless be believed.

"I don't think so," said Orla. "But your thought about his telling the whole colluding group…that is another good theory. Christopher, you don't know the names of the regular men in that party other than the organizer, do you?"

"On the whole, no, unless they paid for something extra, or stayed the night. Your Tate was in that category—bought one of those oversize bottles for the party. Showing off to hide his embarrassments, I bet."

"Would you please not call him 'my Mr. Tate,' as I wish him to the very devil!"

The men reared back, and out of the corner of her eye, Orla saw Olive duck her head, looking at the ground. Was that a— smile?

"Now, names. Christopher, if you could search your records for any of the other names, I'd be obliged. How many men would you say were there each time?"

"Six, sometimes seven."

"Oh, well, that doesn't sound so bad as I was thinking."

"Bad enough," O'Brien announced, grumpy.

"We'll try to track down the seven, including Ormond who made the reservation, and Tate who was a sometimes guest. But what will we tell them to make me not worth coming after?"

Another silence.

"We have the power of the press at our disposal, once we find any proof. That is good leverage. But…" O'Brien looked at her sadly. "We don't have it."

"Perhaps Mr. McNary will know things about them? Or the other reporters at the meeting?"

"If we had names, perhaps." They all turned to Christopher, who cringed.

"I'll try," he said apologetically. "They are all cotton importers, no? That's a pool—"

"A rather large one, I'm afraid, Mr. Rafferty. But it is helpful."

They nodded at one another, each trying to bolster the others up with a hopeful look.

"Can I stay to help Aunt Smith?" came Olive's voice. Her father looked over, surprised.

"What's this?" he said.

"At least for the night. She's still recovering!"

"I think you're getting rather too carried away with the excitement of this *confidential conference,* Olive. Now—"

"I'm ashamed to say she is right, Christopher. I am still hobbling about, and she would be a great help. If you and Serena could spare her the one night, or two? I'll bring her back myself, of course."

"But—is it safe?"

"I think," she darted a glance at O'Brien, who blinked slowly in agreement, "that I am safe here, and so she is safe here."

Christopher blew out a big breath. "Well! Brought a child I didn't expect to bring, leaving a child I didn't expect to leave! There's gratitude for you." But he was already pulling his daughter up into a hug. "Now prove yourself worthy of your task, Olive. Careful attention and discreet movements, yes?"

After another moment embracing his daughter, he turned to Orla.

"I shall look through last year's papers tonight. If you don't bring Olive back tomorrow, I'll be round the next day with any papers I have."

"Good. Excellent thought. Thank you, brother."

"Of course." They shook hands warmly and he walked out with purpose. Orla paused to exhale some of her nervousness about the meeting before addressing Mr. O'Brien.

"Do you think I've got it right?"

"About your friend and her new husband? I don't know. But it sounds like you've thought it through pretty well. What I'm wondering..." He glanced at Olive meaningfully. "...is if you are safe here. If it is your friend, why wouldn't she tell them where you live?"

"Maybe their message is, 'stay where you are, stay out of our business,' and they just mean to draw a line and scare me out of calling attention to their bad practices."

O'Brien nodded slowly, contemplating, and chewed his lip. "And if that is the case, we have no choice but to carry the game to their field." He gathered himself up and stood. He turned to Olive and truly looked at her for the first time.

"Olive, is it? Well. I'm glad your aunt has a companion close by tonight. You take good care of her. We shall do our part, too."

"Yes, sir."

With a tip of his hat, he was gone. Orla felt all the starch go out of her. Before she could let the shaking in her hands get worse, she rose, again pushing off the arms of the chair. It was getting better. She pulled upward on the window sash until a hand's width showed out into the night.

"Aunt? Shouldn't we—"

"Just wait."

And within five minutes, a ginger cat wriggled its way under the window. He jumped down and shook.

Orla smiled. "You look magnificent, Lev. Thank you for coming so promptly." She shut the window firmly and twitched the curtains closed.

"Now! Tell me about yourself, Olive."

Chapter 33

Orla had a lot of time to think about things that night, since once she lay down, she couldn't get back up without help or a lot of pain. She lay in her bed, listening to the slow, even breathing of her niece next to her. She saw a whole series of shadow visions play out on her wall portraying the points in her life where she might have chosen differently.

Could she have chosen differently?

There was her insistence on working at the manse, in order to be less of a burden on her family as the eldest child. That had been expected, and she'd been proud, if a little scared, to do it.

There was her kindness to Robert, who had been so shy and self-effacing at first that she hadn't known he was flirting. Then when she did realize, she had a moment to balance all her previous expectations against all the new sensations she *might* have. That is where her father would have had her choose differently.

But she had loved Robert. The chance he offered her, the steadiness he promised her, that was worth leaving the Church. And what they'd discovered together over the years: patience, affection, understanding, pride—it *had* been worth it.

But his death left her to negotiate all those things all over again.

If she went back to the family she still had, need she go back to the Church?

No, what would the Church want with me? I'm an outsider now.

If she saw someone without integrity, could she continue working with them?

No, I had to take a stand with Gittlings and learn how to handle my own money.

But her first attempt to do so had landed her in hot water. And now she was scrambling.

If only I'd had the time to make the decisions I did later, without the disastrous side trip to the Oswald firm. Grant had managed to get her shares back in order after a few weeks, but the damage had already been done. Thank goodness she had made a good bundle out of Oswald, then chosen well with the other firms.

I'm glad to understand the investment schemes better. And the way that newspapers report things. And how Parliament can be influenced.

Could that be it?

The shadow visions gave way to hazier images as Orla imagined event after event. When she finally settled on a plan of action, she fell asleep instantly.

The next morning she woke up to a cheerful fire and the smell of ginger. *Ginger?*

"Olive?" she called.

No answer.

She struggled to rise, and ended up rolling to her side then slithering off the bed. *Ah! That's how it's done!*

She splashed her face with water from the bowl and rinsed her mouth. By the time she had put on her warm dressing gown and opened the back door, Olive was just a few feet away, tramping over the lawn. She stopped at the sudden motion of the door, then smiled so broadly Orla couldn't help answering with her own.

"Good morning, Aunt."

"Good morning, Olive. What have you got there?"

She had one of Orla's aprons on, and the pocket held a bundle of something.

"You'll see. Have you had breakfast yet?"

Orla remembered the ginger. "What did you make? I hadn't been home in three days, what was there to—"

"You had some ginger syrup, but I knew that was very dear, so I only used a little to put in some breakfast rolls. They're the only ones I know to do blind, and I figured I could just swap out the sugar syrup for ginger syrup," she said shyly.

"It smells very good, I'm glad you're here to have some with me." Orla brought her in for a careful embrace. "But what have you got in my apron?"

"Oh! The comfrey I was talking about. I also asked the grocer for some almond oil, on your account, to make a bitty salve."

"Olive!"

The girl drew back immediately. "Yes?"

"Don't be frightened! I'm just surprised at all your initiative. I had no idea you knew how to do all these things. You're a very grown-up—" she stopped herself in time to amend her original intent. "—young woman. I'm sure your parents are very proud of you."

After Orla tasted a bite of her roll, she looked at Olive with a surprised grin. "And I am very proud of your baking ability, though I have naught to do with it. These are divine!"

Olive beamed, blushed, and they continued chatting about favorite recipes. When Olive moved to test her salve over the fire, she went silent.

"Aunt?"

"Mm?"

"Are you in trouble because you broke the law?"

Orla sighed. "No, my girl. I did overhear a private conversation. I did use that knowledge to make a financial decision. That is not, strictly speaking, illegal. Though I wish I hadn't," she added. "No, it is because after that I changed my mind, moved my money, and then published why—the lies those charlatans were telling to the public. So now they are angry and they want to punish me. I think part of it is because I'm a woman, and shouldn't be sticking my nose in."

Which, fair enough, for the overhearing part, she chided herself.

"But that's no call to knock someone down in the street. I want to stand up to them. And now I have a plan."

"Does it involve that great lummock Mr. O'Brien?"

"Olive!"

"Only he is a great big fellow, and anyone can see he's sweet on you."

"I don't see anything of the sort!" Orla huffed a bit, her dignity fluttering like a tattered sail. "No, no. It will involve some of my friends here and some of them in the south. Honestly, you shouldn't go around calling people names like that."

"It's not a bad name, is it? He's just got big shoulders, and a chest like a barrel, and—"

"That is quite enough; don't make me take back my words about being grown-up."

After a short silence, the salve was set aside to cool. Orla made tea for them both, then sat down to write her letters of action.

Chapter 34

The letters were sent, and Orla was staying in the village that week, except for the journey she made to escort Olive home after a day of getting to know her.

The salve had helped, and she deserved to be acknowledged for it. When they arrived at the inn, she made a point of enumerating Olive's thoughtful and decisive actions to her mother.

"Well, I'm glad she was helpful. I near had an attack when I found her gone, til Christopher's note."

"It's a lovely cottage, Mam. Just the kind I would like one day," said Olive.

A look passed between Orla and Serena. Not exactly the sort of solitude they hoped for a girl of tender years.

"Yes, well, there are many paths a girl can take in life, and mine started off with a lot of hard work, you mustn't forget that part, hmm?"

Serena tried to hide her smile.

"No, Aunt."

The reunion made Orla feel good, however. She was bolstered by the girl's confidence as she went to find her brother and see what he'd found in his receipts. She was not as pleased with his greeting.

"Ah! Orla. Still upright, I see."

Her glare made his charming smile falter.

"I only meant—"

"I'm doing fine, thank you. And you?"

The quick smile again. "Well. And good news."

"Oh?" The glare lifted.

"I found one other name only, but," he paused for effect. Her brother should have had a career on the stage. "The pattern is clear. Here, look."

He showed her the names he'd put on a list. Then he took out a map with X's placed on several points by the river. Orla peered closer, her neck much better able to function now. She sent up a prayer of gratitude for Olive's comfrey salve.

"So I've marked off the eight places I think may be related. One may not be, but I'm not sure which one, since these all seem to be in the same importing categories and likely to be associates. One of them, however, must have declined to participate."

"Interesting."

"Yes, isn't it," her brother commented. "Perhaps another firm ripe for investing, if you can tell who it is, outside the pale here."

"Yes. This is very helpful, Christopher. Thank you. May I borrow this?"

"Of course. Come here." He embraced her gingerly. "I'm sorry for the gibe. I do worry for you, it's just...how it comes out, I suppose."

"I know." Her soft response was muffled further by being said into his shoulder, but he understood. They parted and he bit his lip.

"Who else will you enlist for scouting out the firms? You mustn't go alone."

"No," she agreed. "I've got a plan. Don't you worry, brother o' mine." She smiled briefly. "And how is Father doing?"

"Better still. I told him of what happened to you—just the injury, not all the rest. He worries for you too, you know." Orla sighed.

"As *we* worry about *him*. But…"

"I know," Christopher said. In his look was understanding and forgiveness and acknowledgement.

She squeezed his hand once more before returning home.

While she did not venture into Town that week, the notes Orla sent did summon Town to her. Mr. McNary came to call on Wednesday, bearing messages.

"Mr. Grant sends his best wishes for your recovery, along with this restorative jelly from his cook." The earnest man brandished the basket he'd been hiding behind his back.

"Oh, do thank Mr. Grant in person for me. Thank you, Mr. McNary." She took the basket and unpacked the cloth-wrapped jelly carefully. "It does look very fine."

"Yes, I've been inhaling its fumes in the coach. Then there is this note from Mr. O'Brien." He reached into his coat pocket and proffered the envelope, sealed with green wax. Orla colored slightly, Olive's comments looming in her mind.

"Thank you. You're quite the messenger today." She took the letter but forebore opening it, merely holding it in her lap as she sat and indicated for McNary to do the same at her small table.

"I could hope to be a little more useful than that, but since I am the one here, I trust there is more to be done?"

"Much. I need you to rack your brains for me about several names so we can narrow our search. So here—"

She set aside O'Brien's envelope and spread Christopher's map over the table. She tapped each location in succession and listened as McNary listed off all he knew of each company's activities and connections. She took copious notes over the thirty or forty minutes they spent in this manner, careful to keep her competent but inelegant script legible, in case she needed to pass these notes on. In case she couldn't investigate them herself.

When they were done, they'd decided on who their outlier was 'beyond the pale' of the illegal selling, and Orla determined to broach the subject with him for help in the matter: Bodkins, who collected woolens from the lowlands and the ridings to export, was the one who did not fit, and who might turn out to be a good investment and ally.

She and McNary shook hands after sharing a glass of sherry and a slice of the jelly—it did indeed taste very nice—and he went on his way. Orla sat down, her skin tingling with—what? Danger? Excitement? Suddenly she just wanted rest, and made for her own bed.

The cat stood on the threshold. When it saw her, it started complaining fiercely.

"Apologies, I didn't forget you, shhh! Hold on, Lev," she said as she scurried back into the kitchen. A plate of the jelly and a dish of milk were duly served up. Orla fell asleep before the cat could come and thank her, unsurprisingly.

Chapter 35

The next stage of the plan took longer, dictated by the Royal Mails and Parliamentary procedure. The sessions were well underway by the time she'd got her requests to her friends Burch and Darcy. They had to talk to their caucus leaders before getting on the schedule, then prepare their alliances while they waited. Orla imagined it all from Glasgow, not being willing to travel all that way to witness Parliament's inaction in person.

She heard about the first victory in a letter from Elizabeth:

"I should have known Clever You would come back with a subtler and more substantial victory than beating someone senseless in the street! I ache for your pain and fear, my friend, and I am wickedly glad that the blackguards are to be squeezed in this way. Here is how Darcy has engineered the changes..."

And here Elizabeth went into some of the minutiae of procedure necessary to wrap a noose around the misbehaving companies. An admonishment, a censure, a withdrawal of license, and a hefty fine were all levied against firms who misrepresented their goods and were found guilty at the assizes. Her friend really seemed to be enjoying this part more than Orla was, and she smiled at the thought. Elizabeth always was good at the sly retort.

"…and if you are still hiding in your poor cottage, please come to pay us a visit. The children will be pleased and while it may be a few dreadful days for travel, we are having a fine spring here, you would love the feel of the air."

Orla tucked this note away in her desk and considered. She had going concerns here, but she also needed to be cautious about her travels. Could she go away without endangering her new projects? She couldn't have imagined how woven into the fabric of other people's lives she would be only two years after losing her husband, but now…

The cat ran by, chasing a reflection in the glass.

And there is the cat to consider now, she thought, smiling wider.

When could she consider herself clear of the danger? When would it truly be finished? Though Darcy had done her a towering favor by getting some action from the law, it did not put them in jail or shackle their hands. Would it not be merely the batting of the lion's nose, enraging him to attack harder? This was why she needed Burch's reply before she made her decision. Would she be free?

Lev raced back again.

Free. Her thoughts turned to the negotiations going on currently for how to finance Parliament's compensations to the slaveholders, the planters. She thought about Tate and his wealth generated by years and years of slavery in sugar. About his desperate attempts to keep the status symbols of his position, even through shameful means. Did he regret his actions now? Might he respond to reason?

She didn't dare trust to that yet. Deciding she needed the trip to stay to the Darcys even without Burch's report, she pulled Elizabeth's note back out and wrote her reply.

"Dearest Elizabeth,

Thank you for your delicious and wicked note of the 2nd. Thank you for all you have done, and be sure to thank Mr. Darcy as well as you know how. This does ease my mind considerably, and I accept your offer to visit with pleasure. I like this air you speak of. Crookston's has been very violent and soggy of late. But tell me, would your offspring tolerate the presence of a visiting feline?"

It was while Orla was in Northumberland for her stay of several weeks that she received the third piece of news. The cat had not liked the coaches at all, and the basket she'd carried him in was now shredded past repair. But once on the estate, he became once again the happy, curious git she now loved.

The children did, in fact, take to him, likely because they had just lost their friendly barn cat. Orla stood in the shelter of a large willow to watch the children at play one April afternoon, shouting encouragement to whichever sibling had lost the shuttlecock. She was well placed to observe the rider thunder up the drive, wheel his mount to the side, hand off a sack to the waiting butler, and disappear just as quickly.

"Chestnut," the boy Colin said proudly.

"With dapples," his sister Marianne corrected him.

The pause in play was broken, and they resumed, until they saw Orla set off for the house.

"It's the post," Marianne said. "Let's go in."

"I knew that," Colin insisted, following with their dawdling sister Lily.

At one point, Orla turned back to make sure they were following. *I almost left them alone. Can I be that worried?*

Yes, came the answer. *Yes, you certainly can.*

As soon as she was able, Orla procured the letter for herself and stole away to read it in private, trusting the staff to know what was best for their beloved charges. It was from O'Brien.

Mrs. Smith,

I have insinuated myself with uncanny charm into the necessary circle. Well, some of them are in the circle. Uncanny charm is not the best way to introduce oneself, but necessity hurried my hand. At any rate, I have secured the assurances of a prominent justice to attend to the matter for which I have placed the evidence, our sworn affidavits, in his hands. He has an able deputy, known to me to be astute, which helps our cause tremendously.

In addition, upon hearing your ambition to start piece-meal shares for the workers on the river, he admires the idea much and wishes to speak with you on the topic, next time you are in London. I did not wish to speak for you, but recommended he write you himself with the support. Justice Gibbons is going over the evidence and the brief from the court now. We await his decision to accompany the bailiffs back north, before which I will assuredly send you notice.

Yours most assuredly,

Jas. Bronterre O'Brien

The paper was flickering. Her hands were shaking. Was this it? Could she piece her life back together in a few weeks' time? That idea she'd had for the joint shares—he'd remembered that from perhaps the second time they'd met, when she'd advanced the idea at a meeting of the reporters. She felt a queer little lurch under her ribs, and reminded herself to breathe.

Elizabeth's knock, soft and rapid, sounded on her door.

"Come away in," Orla said softly.

"Come away, is it? What's sent you back into the past, my dear?"

For while Orla had not shared her Catholic past with Isobel, she had done with Elizabeth, her first friend as a married person. She knew the accent she'd long ago polished away.

"It is good news, but I—I am afraid to feel relief quite yet."

"I know exactly what you mean. It is so every time a friend goes through childbirth." Elizabeth paused, thoughtful. "Does the current trouble bring back the worries from when you were a girl?"

"You mean money worries? No, not exactly." Orla remembered the ache in the pit of her stomach when their family had been together: together, but usually hungry, often cold. The uneasiness she felt was higher, nestled under where her ribs met, and more of a curling sensation than a weight. She didn't bother trying to explain such nonsense.

"It's more about freedom, I suppose. Can I walk about as I wish? See whom I wish? Associate with whom I wish? It was heady, when I first came out of mourning, to be allowed so much...but then, it disappeared."

"I see. You don't want to take it for granted."

Orla nodded, looking out the window. Realizing she still held O'Brien's letter, she folded it and put it away in her valise.

"Well, I don't feel taken for granted," Elizabeth replied with a bit more force. "And doubt others in your life would either. Here's to a rising future, increased welfare and expanded freedoms!" They weren't holding cups, so instead of a toast, Elizabeth grabbed her hands and twirled her around. Laughing, Orla twisted her arms for her friend to execute the same move.

"That's settled, then," Elizabeth said, dark eyes sparkling.

Chapter 36

How many people had to help? Orla blenched at the thought of all the people she did not know, could not thank, would always owe, unknowing. She trembled at it, but it made her more determined to proceed with her new idea. Now that she need no longer fear that 'gang,' as she'd taken to calling the group of seven colluders in her head, she was forging ahead with organizing plans.

No more ferrying around petitions. No more sending for soup. Those were both important needs being fulfilled, but she had found a different niche that needed *her* to be filled. And that felt marvelous.

When May arrived, she sent three of her dresses to be modified—updated to the latest trend—and she refreshed her store of necessary undergarments as well. She liked this rotation. She also finally assented to Amelia's request to visit her in Manchester, and to write to the address they had for her uncle. Her father had not yet brought himself to do it, and she found she didn't want to wait for precedence to light the way. Not in this new year of 1834, when so many other barriers were being pushed away.

While these threads of her personal life were being restrung, she turned to McNary and the library once again to set up a base of expertise. Jamieson recommended a broker, McLean brought in a legal scholar, and her reliable Mr. Grant orchestrated several key transactions to line up the pins perfectly. Now, with the elite bankers running around scared because of government debt and risky loans, she had the elbow room to maneuver, thanks to Scotland's still-loose banking regulations.

Orla sat tall in her seat at the head of the table. She waited in what had turned into their board-room over the past months: a rented room in a discussion hall known as Temple Weston, hard by Threadneedle Street and convenient for most of their journalist allies.

Her hands were folded on the table, a single paper with her reminders written out in front of her. She wore her deep plum velvet jacket, which felt comfortable but business-like, and gave her confidence. As her eyes stared without seeing, the door to the room opened slowly, as if the opener hesitated.

"Hello?" came a man's voice.

"Hello," Orla returned.

He came round the door and saw her, his round face going rounder with a pleasant smile. "Ah! Mrs. Smith." His slight Germanic accent gave his identity away.

"Mr. Hess?" When he nodded, she indicated for him to sit down with her. "Welcome. I hear you are a genius at actuarial science."

"Oh, nothing much…" His ears went a little red. Orla bit her lip. If they were all so easily readable, that would make her interviewing easy, but security for their group that much harder.

"I am happy to have specialists on board, Mr. Hess, when we want to know the most up-to-date practices for our bank to keep it safe and secure. How do you do?"

Before he could vouchsafe an answer, someone knocked on the door. Mr. Hess jumped up. Orla did not. The next gentleman entered, spotted immediately because of his perfectly coiffed hair, let alone his expensive suit and boots that shone. Mr. Hess made an unconscious movement toward his own mop of hair. Orla inclined her head.

The gentleman introduced himself to the room.

"Rosebery, at your service."

"Good afternoon, my lord. Thank you both for coming. My Lord Rosebery, this is Mr. Hess, our accountancy expert."

They bowed to one another. One by one, other men entered, until they had all been introduced or introduced themselves in undertones, and the crowd of eight quite filled the room around the long table.

"Gentlemen, please be seated." Orla smiled to disarm them. It worked on a few. "I am here to help those less fortunate, as are you. I have learned recently that we have a window of time open to us to enact a new kind of investment scheme that may benefit those artisans, miners, factory workers, and more— those who work and yet because of the price of daily food have nothing left to show for their efforts. I believe this is a failing of our system, and I hope you see it this way too."

She scanned their eyes as she said this, looking for any recalcitrance, and nerves that gave the owner away. Nothing.

"Most of you have experience with the joint stock system. It is new, it is ill-understood, and little regulated. What we need for the poor workers is something that counters the part of the joint stock company. What if," and she changed her tone from one of a preacher exhorting to that of a friend tempting. "Instead of one man holding many shares and directing an enterprise, it was many men holding one share, and having a proportional vote?"

So far this was ground they knew. Each man had been informed of the purpose of the meeting and come willingly due to contacts or connections, strong-armed by an aunt in one particular case. But for the details, they were hanging on her every word.

"I do not say that each owner of a partial share should have the same vote as a sole owner, but we can apply the mathematical proportions and compute a partial vote. What is important is that they feel invested, they are learning how to forecast, how to persuade, and hearing others do so. And they are not putting all their eggs in one basket, to have it cruelly swept away by chance."

"I think this is how we raise workers out of the poverty that the new currency and banking flows have left them in. This Empire—" and here she glanced at her paper so as not to misstep, "—this Empire has changed how it views its citizens. It had changed our relations to one another. And so a new way of supporting each other must emerge as well. Or we face more risings, rebellions, and riots."

"This instrument is something we can use as a bank, which is how you can help. We file papers as a bank. A small one, to start, and concerned with assembling these partial shares and putting the money in solid investments. To distribute the risk, we choose ten firms, and two shares in each. At an average of three pounds per share, so sixty pounds, we would need to assemble three hundred sixty in order to make the purchase a reasonable four shillings for the working man."

Several of the gentlemen's faces were creased in computation. Orla paused, the long speech unnerving her a bit. She squeezed her toes in her boots so that the tension would not show on her face. Once their expressions had eased again, she continued with the financing and licensing plans.

Yes, it would cost them money, she thought while speaking. But that would keep them honest, no? They had been vetted for good character, and there was no way she could see of their diverting funds for their own gain. She'd asked. At many different bank branches, she'd surreptitiously researched this plan, with McNary's help, since O'Brien stayed in London.

"I'm sure you have questions, but your fellow men may be better able to answer than I can, so I would suggest we circle the table…" She led a civilized but animated discussion of how to start this bank, how to recruit, how to finance, what their policies should be, what their investments should be, and more, for two hours. When they had finally wound down, still musing but satisfied, Orla finally stood.

"Thank you, gentlemen. The only item left is the name. We'll take suggestions at our next directors' meeting, in two weeks." She smiled to soften the dismissal. There was a low chuckle of humor, and she let the approbation ease her jellied limbs.

One man approached her and she braced herself. It was Lord Rosebery.

"This has been well prepared, Mrs. Smith. You have much to be proud of." She acknowledged this with a nod, wondering what was coming. "I wonder if I might invite another member into the board—"

Orla was already shaking her head when she heard his next syllable.

"—She is very much as detail-minded as you are, and has been trained to tally accounts and project earnings on several of the farms I own. She would be a steward if it were not for her sex, and..."

"And?" Orla scrutinized his long, narrow face.

"She is of mixed parentage, from St. Kitts. She is in fact a cousin, but unacknowledged outside the family circle. You understand..."

I very much do. "I see. An unusual arrangement, but perhaps a unique and useful set of skills, as well. I would very much like to meet her. Does she live nearby?"

"She stays in Fife for the most part, but I can request her attendance, say in one week?" Without seeking further agreement, he bowed, so Orla was forced to curtsy.

"She's very good with bestowing names, too, so I shall pass along the information, if I may?"

"Certainly, but my lord, you haven't told me *her* name."

"Ah! Esther Primrose, madam. I look forward to our next meeting."

All at once, the tension went out of Orla's muscles and her bowels felt like water. She went out to find the water closet but was met by McNary, coming in like a sneak-thief.

"How did it go?" he fairly whispered.

"They're all gone, I think. And—if you would excuse me one minute, Mr. McNary, I must attend to something, but would like to speak with you shortly?"

He acknowledged and found a seat to wait while she found the necessary on an upper floor. *The relief!*

Much more relaxed and refreshed, Orla returned to the meeting room.

"I observed them as they were leaving, our Gang of Seven," he said cheekily. "They looked thoughtful, contemplative, curious—all good frames of mind. I'd say it went well based on that. How do you feel about it?"

"They were very astute; we chose well. Their questions were encouraging. Also, Lord Rosebery asked to bring on a—" She didn't know if she had been told in confidence about the family connection. It was quite a striking admission from a stranger. "—an employee from one of his estates to help choose the investments. She," she emphasized the syllable, "is mixed-race."

McNary's eyebrow raised. She continued after registering his reaction.

"I'm very curious what sort of person such a man would put forward, and I'm meeting her in one week. I expect he'll send me a note when she comes to town from Fife. The imperious sort, as you'd expect."

McNary chuckled. "Fascinating. I hope she turns out to be an asset to the project. Now, shall I tell you the latest from the *Bankers Circular*?"

McNary became rather a gossiping magpie for the next half hour as they sat together discussing the new developments.

"We shall have to incorporate quickly," Orla said. "I did not expect the government to move so fast."

"Nor I. But the month should be fast enough. Well, good luck, my dear. Shall I see you on Monday?"

"Yes," she said, and squeezed his hand in recognition. The friends parted to carry out their respective missions.

Chapter 37

Orla could speak of none of her plans to the sisters in Crookston village, but that did not stop her from inviting them over for supper that Saturday evening. Betsy's talk was of the tactics of the drovers coming up for the spring, while Louise's measured contributions were of the news she heard from her correspondents in the far corners of the island.

In her turn, Orla shared what she knew of the political scene from her newspaper contacts. The conversation had just turned to medlar recipes when Lev rose from his perch and went to stare out the window, his back arching and the hairs standing on end.

Alerted by this unusual behavior, Orla went to look covertly, never mind that her guests saw her do it.

She saw no one.

It was only when she turned to see them both looking at her, frozen in mid-speech, that she realized it was such a mistake.

"The cat," she said. "I was worried it was a prowler, after my knock on the head—or neck, rather."

They relaxed, immediately more solicitous once they understood her anxiety.

"I'm sure it's nothing."

"Cats are always starting at nothing."

"He is a cheeky little fellow, isn't he?"

"Yes," Orla smiled. "He is. I like it when he's here, and I don't mind it when he's gone."

"Best arrangement, really," Betsy said, elbowing her sister.

They finished their visit and the women went back to their cottage, Orla still scanning the surrounding fields as they left for indications all was not normal. But it looked completely normal, and she was forced to give up the exercise and retire, without the cat, to bed.

A few days later, Orla did indeed receive the note from the lord she had expected. His employee, Esther Primrose would see her at her address at six the next evening, or wherever was convenient. She replied in the affirmative and went about her necessary tasks in preparation.

Esther arrived in a bit of rain, with a modest dress and a stout umbrella. When she entered her home, Orla saw her efforts at neatness with the bonnet, the well-tailored coat, and the tucked-up hairstyle. Her skin was the same color taupe as the tea she liked, when her milk and sugar were added.

They introduced themselves and Orla served tea with a rich tea bread and jam. After the niceties had been observed, she broke the ice.

"Do you know why Lord Rosebery sent you here?"

Orla saw her shoulders raise quickly, as if jerking in reaction. She held onto the biscuit in her hand, however.

"Not exactly. I know he's promised my relatives he'd look for a more professional post for me, but it is difficult for a woman to find a position that uses too much of her brain, wouldn't you agree, Mrs. Smith?"

The slight lilting tones of her voice were very pleasant, and Orla almost lost the sense of the words as she listened to their melody. She performed her own jerk of the shoulders, coming back to the question, remembering her duty.

"In many cases, yes. Could you tell me about the work you do for Mr. Primrose currently?" She listened to the litany of small tasks, nodding in acknowledgement of her competence.

"And your ambitions?"

There, the woman looked taken aback, and no wonder. By so many of the categories that society filters out of their lists of 'Ambitious People', Esther would be excluded. She was a woman, she was Black, she was older, she was not temptingly beautiful. But she did have a strong head for assessing risk and trusting people, and she had been well protected at Lord Rosebery's for eight years. It was time she launch herself into society: if not as a debutante, then as a canny business owner.

Orla's brows shot up but she encouraged her to go on to present her story.

"Lord Rosebery says he told you there was a family connection." Orla nodded. "It was his father, who was my mother's father, back on St. Kitts. My mother and I grew up working in the kitchens of their estate. And back then—well, the old Lord suffered nobody to step a foot outside their place, is what. Until he died, and the present Lord had to look in on things, came from Liverpool special just to do so. And he saw the lay of the land, both there and here. He talked with my mother—siblings! And he agreed to take me here for school, though—" She looked away briefly. "Though the schools for people like me here are not much better than the ones there. Until I found the Quakers."

Esther smiled for the first time, lighting up her whole face. "I see," Orla said, though she did not.

"In London," she amended. "There are some enlightened school opportunities here but I was in London."

"And so now you run the farm accounts in Fife?" Orla was a little lost why Rosebery had sent this woman to her.

"My ambitions," she continued, as if Orla had not spoken. "If I were a man, I think I would be a politician." Her frankness intrigued Orla. "If I were viewed as white, that is. I suppose a Black man might earn a post as a steward… But I can be neither of these things. Where my ambitions lie—to be powerful enough to change history! With those who rebel, but live to fight another day! Too many of the people I saw fight for liberty were murdered. Killed, like mad dogs. I know respectability here is not an iron suit of armor—but the distance helps it become a better shield. It is why I made sure to learn the pianoforte while I studied in London."

Orla's eyes were glistening after hearing her passion, and then she laughed out loud. The pianoforte, indeed. She suddenly had all sorts of feelings surging, questions pressing on her—she felt her breath coming in fast gulps and made a point to close her mouth and breathe deeply.

"A better shield," she repeated. Lord Rosebery had said she was good with names. "You may have just named our bank. I would love to ask you about piano lessons, but first, whom should we ask for capital—something tells me you have ideas."

Chapter 38

McNary

While Orla pursued the directors end, Oscar McNary was out with a journalist friend of his, going house to house hearing from weavers, bricklayers, thread spinners, bleachers, masons, and yes, miners. They were transmitting the message that there would be investment opportunities to help the free unstamped press, and he was emboldened to see that many of them knew they were allies in the fight for labor.

"Sure, we was all in by the tea urn listenin' to yer man the patterer, and he sayin' all the stories of the great speeches in the fields. We know where the just stand."

Words like this made Oscar feel again! It had been so long since he had been out doing this sort of work; others had been canvassing for him for nigh on a decade. But meeting his fellow man, in all the decrepitude of his housing, in the dank state of his clothes, in the bare state of his cupboard, made McNary humble in the face of their mission.

"The great speeches in the field! Did you make your way to any of them, my friend?"

"Aye, one came as near as Cambernauld, sir, and we all of us went from the village. My wife and children, too. It was O'Connor who spoke that day, sir, and he said only what was right. What should be ours."

"'Struth, and weren't that some six or seven year ago?" another man called from the street. Oscar looked around to find himself and his friend the center of a loose ring of interested folk, a few fellows mixed in with faded women with children on their hip. "What's happened since then, eh? Piss all."

"The children can go to school now, Dick," protested one woman.

"The wages are still shot," he fired back.

"Yes," Oscar fairly yelped. "And that is why a money strategy is what we need. Money is what they listen to."

After a fraction of a pause, Dick's dirt-streaked face creased into a grin. "I wager you've the way of it," he said.

Geographic progress was slow, as this sort of congregating happened every few houses. But the way Oscar felt in his heart —it was leaps and bounds above what it had been that morning.

Another day, one house held only a woman, and they were going to turn away, but she called them back.

"Ain't you been causin' the ruckus down the way?"

Oscar and Jack looked at each other and shrugged.

"Maybe, ma'am. Which ruckus would this be?"

She eyed them from under a thick red plaid which she wore partially over her head, partially draped across her shoulders.

"Tryin' to take poor people's money," she accused. "An' them goin' along wi'it!!"

"It's four shillings, a reasonable amount to save up for, ma'am, and we're investing our own in the same way. This is better than the free soup, I'm tellin' ye. We can grow power this way, and hold onto it!"

Oscar let Jack speak, gambling that his accent would be more trusted. He didn't know if the woman had family or was working, but he wanted to convince her anyway. He broke in.

"The problem with the rich in power is they can direct the law to do their bidding, don't you think?"

"Aye..." she said cautiously.

"But the law is made by people who have a stake, or people who are directed by those who have a stake. It is changing from land to other wealth—the source of power of many in the Commons today is industry—manufactures! And if we can join that crowd with our own Members, we can direct the law just as well, wouldn't you say?"

She wasn't taking kindly to his cajoling.

"You don't think land matters anymore, do you? Well, let me tell you, it would have made a difference if we had it, twenty year ago." Her voice got lower, snapping like a leather whip through air. "If we'd been able to hang onto our land, we'd not have ended up beggars and laborers, trapped in this city, everything owned by some grand bounder. It's force—they forced us off, and that's the only t'ing that will answer them back. Whether it be force of the law, the sheriffs, or the mob of us—" Her voice went a bit ragged. Oscar wanted to put an arm out to assist her, but he was slight and she was substantial, with the shoulders of a washer woman. He waited while she caught her breath instead.

"Aye, it may be that money weighs more than land in the Commons these days, but that's only now that we're all dependents. We need that money, mister, for food and heat and shoes." The fire seemed to have gone out of her, but Oscar was touched.

"Ma'am, do you have family that live with you? Will they return soon?"

She gave a grim smile. "I do. They may return, but I doubt much 'twill be soon. My two sons went for soldiers and my two daughters to service. I let to boarders now, two again, and they eat up every penny they pay me. It is...surviving. Good luck to ye, sir."

She closed the door, shutting it tight as if he weren't there. And for her, he wasn't. His flying spirits flagged a little. Then he reminded himself that for those who had been crushed, others had to take up the banner. They pushed on to the next house.

Chapter 39

Christopher

He wondered sometimes how she'd sorted everything out, his sister. Last autumn, there'd been that snooty couple that stopped in to threaten him and his, over something Orla was meddling in. He hadn't gone to her right away, and when he had, she'd listened carefully, gone quiet, then apologized to him. Apologized! As if he were a stranger.

Christopher had seen she had a plan, at least, when he finally did visit, at her request. But she did not confide in him. It made him wonder, in turn, about her husband, old Robert. Had she kept everything inside for those fourteen years? Or had she had an equal as helpmeet, as he considered his Serena? He and Lennán had talked recently, too, about all the siblings.

As his oldest son, Christopher heard out his father's requests for when he died, and read the will he'd made. Neither of them thought it was an immediate concern, but one only lived so long in a city like Glasgow.

"And you've written to the priest for permission? You're sure you've still got a space for the family at St. Anne's?"

"Aye," said his father. They sat outside his father's tenement, in the small, bare yard formed by the walls round the privy at the back. Two graying crates, usually used for the man with his pipe of tobacco, did service as their seats.

"Who's the priest now, then?" It wasn't that he wanted to challenge his father. He was curious.

"Tis the same man, by God, will ye let me get on with it?"

"Sorry, Da."

"Elspeth is content to move back when I go. Seeing as you're established, it makes sense to leave any money I have for her to bring up young Ian and Marie."

"Of course." Christopher thought it was more a case of no savings being had, but didn't dispute the point. If Elspeth and the children needed money to find a home back in Wexford after the funeral, he'd find it for them.

· "Orla wrote to Murchadh," Lennán said abruptly. Christopher had to reconnect the two names in his head for the first time. His sister had written to his uncle?

"Murchadh, your brother?" Christopher pronounced it the English way, closer to 'Murrow.' He hadn't grown up with the Gaelic. Lennán nodded tersely. "When?"

"Couple months past. She told me when she did it. To give me the chance to do it first, I suppose." The old man didn't say anything for a few seconds, and the smacking of his gums was the only sound added to the street's general hubbub of dusk.

"It surprised me, but it shouldn't," he settled on at last. "She's a good colleen, will best anything or anyone that tries it on." He gave a dry chuckle, then smiled, as serene as Christopher could remember seeing him. "I didn't—don't give her credit enough. But you won't make that mistake, will ye?"

"No, Da."

They'd concluded the serious talk and moved on to politics then. Christopher was more relieved than he could express.

When Christopher recollected the conversation a few days later, worrying about his sister and who she'd gotten involved with, he called Olive to him.

"You've taken a shine to yer auntie, now that she's back in our lives, eh?"

She nodded.

"When you stayed with her a few weeks ago, did you talk things over together, get to know each other?"

She smiled, a little more sure of the conversation. "Yes, Da. I like how she talks to me."

"Aye, well. What did ye talk about?"

Her confident look collapsed, as she scrunched her face up, trying to remember. "She showed me the cottage first, I remember, so I'd know what to look for where. Which was good, since I made breakfast for us the next day. And also went out to get the comfrey for the salve—you know the kind that Auntie—"

"Yes, yes," he cut her off. "I'm not asking for Auntie Mae's receipt for muscle salve, now, m'dear. Did you talk about anything that was...a bit scary, maybe?"

She took her time thinking. Christopher had two children, and he didn't question them closely, as a rule; she was probably nervous or unsure what this was about.

"What I mean is, we know she was staying at home because she was being watched, or followed, or both, and we were all worried about her. Did she seem worried or upset?"

"No, she seemed strong," Olive answered. "She did say a lot about being careful how you choose your friends, which seemed a bit odd...she talked about some lovely friends she had in the south." She turned to him happily. "May I be permitted to accompany her when next Aunt Smith goes south? She said the Burches near London have all sorts of horses, and parties, and—"

Save my poor hide, thought Christopher. "I've no idea about that now, my girl, but I do know we are not the sort to be parading in front of fancy people. You know that. I shall ask Orla about her travel plans next time we see her, but you mustn't get your hopes up. Now: anything else?"

She thought again, her thin jaw in her thin hand, and Christopher was glad they had the tavern from his wife's family to depend on. Finally, Olive lifted her head to gaze at him seriously.

"Aunt Smith did say that she was glad to be visiting us again, and Papa. And that, if she weren't ever to see us again, she'd be very unhappy. It wasn't about anything scary, exactly, but I think she was afraid. Doesn't that sound like something you say if you're worried?"

His heart squeezed. "Aye, it does. All right. That's all I wanted to know, pet. Thank you for racking your brains to remember. And I won't forget to ask about traveling, eh? It's just that being among a certain kind of people requires a certain kind of wardrobe, and that's not the sort of thing we spend our money on, eh?"

"No, sir," she said, resolutely, and not too disappointed.

Regular little soldier after Orla's heart, this one.

Chapter 40

Tate

Aloysius Tate drew himself up, all five feet and five inches of himself. This was most certainly beneath his dignity, but he needed the money, and he needed to instill fear in order to extract the money. He couldn't trust another servant to collect it, since the last one had refused to squeeze the peasants as hard as was required. A Scot! Who would have thought a Scot would have qualms about getting money out of someone?

"If you don't have the money, you'll be put out. I'm making my list now, and going directly to the sheriff." He made an effort to keep his voice low, not let any trace of a whine into it. *Intimidate*, he told himself.

Across from him, framed in the doorway, stood two women blackened with dirt, one a carbon copy of the other, with twenty years' difference between them. A few more ragged children dawdled behind them, but Tate didn't want to have to go in; the stink would no doubt cling to his clothes.

"Mr. Tate, sir, we got all we could selling our furniture, but we need to keep the bed so we don't catch the damp. The babies, sir—"

"How much?"

"Eighteen shillings, Mr. Tate, sir."

"Very well. Hand it over, and I will mark off that much. You'll need to find the—" he consulted his paper, "six shillings remaining by Friday. I'll send my servant. He'll have the same instructions."

"But we have nothing left to sell! How are we to make it to next quarter day if we've nothing for food?" The wretched woman was pleading. Tate sighed.

"It is not my concern." He turned on his heel and tramped through the dust til the next house on his list.

They surrendered the bulk of their wealth, blubbering through the interview. He caught the words 'mother' and 'china' but went off with a lightened step. What business had these ragamuffins to hold on to china, anyway?

The next house and the next were more pitiable scenes, with excuses and extenuating circumstances offered. Tate made the most of his pencil and his list, and got about three-quarters of what he needed to pay Oswald back that month.

Exhausted after several hours of this, he made his way back to the main street where his coach and driver waited, and headed to the river. He dropped his fees, a clerk signed for the amount, and he instructed the coachman to hie them home to Crookston.

Finally, some peace, he thought. *And enjoyment of my wife.*

Only he wasn't allowed to enjoy his wife, for she was up and pacing the floor of the salon, distractedly mouthing words to no one.

"Darling Isobel, what is ailing you? I have just returned triumphant and we can enjoy our meal in peace, if you will calm yourself."

"Calm myself! How can I, when I hear such reports of your indiscreet and," she emphasized the word, "indelicate habits?"

"Oh, what is it now? You won't have me gambling, even though my flash was what appealed to you about me in the first place?" He lowered his eyes and gave her his charming smile.

She aimed an exasperated sigh at him, then smiled. He extended his hand and she came to him. He twirled her round as he'd learned to do in his later lessons, then gripped her waist with a becoming ferocity. When he kissed her, she melted completely in his arms, which relaxed him and excited him. But then—

"Darling, why do I hear dropped hints about your not being able to pay our bills at the shops?"

He thrust her away. "Isobel, do not think I am obliged to answer you. My business is that, *my* business, and you may ask away for all I care. I am handling things my own way. You accepted that when you became my wife. Or is it so long ago you've forgotten?"

"No, sir, I can well remember last year. It is a good memory." She paused. "Only I cut my friend for you, and we made an enemy of her, and now I think that was ill done."

"Good Lord, you do speak your mind freely," he roared, loud enough to imply he wished she wouldn't. She was silent a moment, then hesitating, spoke more quietly.

"I can play the coquette, but I can also speak frankly. You accepted that when you became my husband, did you not? I want to be happy with you, my darling, not vex you. Tell me how to be useful?"

His mind started turning the gears again for an evening's pleasure, but the butler came into the salon after knocking. He looked jumpier than usual.

"Yes?" he said impatiently.

"Some gentlemen to see you, sir."

"Their cards?" He noticed the butler carried no cards, nor tray.

"They—didn't seem to think them necessary. They said they're from the river, sir."

The butler did not meet his eyes but stared resolutely up at the crown molding, as was proper, but Aloysius felt the man's nerves be transmitted to him. *Should I see them alone or with Izzy? I've nothing to hide*, he chided himself. *And she'll mind her own business.*

"Well, show them in."

Isobel's eyes widened—probably from that phrase, 'from the river,' but she moved to sit decorously away from him.

Two men entered. They wore neither cravat nor collar, but buttoned-up jerseys under dark jackets of homespun. Two identical navy blue caps topped their heads and they doffed them slowly when they saw his wife.

"Good day, gentlemen," he said affably. Affability had always helped him avoid difficulties in the past.

"Sir, if we could speak to you in private. We're—" he looked to the other fellow, the one a little shorter.

"Emissaries. From Mr. Oswald."

"We don't want to be no trouble," the taller one said, and bobbed his head toward Izzy.

"I believe our accounts are current," he told them, eyes narrowed as he considered each of them. Knives? Knuckles? What did these ruffians bring? "Why did he think it necessary to send 'emissaries'?"

They fidgeted with their lapels and the shorter one put a hand in his pocket.

Isobel rose quickly, opening her mouth to make some excuse to leave. He cut her off.

"My wife wants to know all my business, so surely a business associate's message can be repeated here, while we are waiting for our refreshment?" He was weighing them against each other, and the knife edge of risk lit him up inside. He would win this round.

"Fine," the taller one said tersely. "Our boss said you're still short and the total must be paid in full by the first of June if you're to get away with what you pulled last summer. That's what we are to relay."

Tate frowned. This is not what he had agreed to, back in that theatre. "But—"

The same man who had spoken reached into his jacket pocket and withdrew a long knife. Before Tate could do more than freeze mid-sentence, he'd sliced through the sofa cushion where his wife had sat before they came in. Black horsehair, wool wadding, and shredded slivers of straw fluttered to the floor.

"Little taste of the damage you might be in for, if you don't satisfy the boss," said the shorter man.

And without another word, they turned and pushed the door open for themselves. The butler was nowhere in sight.

Isobel was white. He thought to comfort her, to turn her eyes away from where they were glued to the torn sofa cushion, but she held up a hand.

"What have you done, Aloysius?" Her voice was low, sharp. Considering this, he realized she might be white with anger, not with fear.

"Darling."

Her eyes flashed up to his, confirming his guess.

"Once we get out of this squeeze, everything will be fine. My father can not live forever, and the lands I am managing are doing well. The wool markets—"

"I don't want to hear about *sheep*, Aloysius. *Who* were they from?"

"What does it matter? They are—"

"They are *dangerous*, you imbecile. I can not believe I married you. I am not staying here to be burnt in my bed."

Tate scoffed. "Where will you go? You have no people, and I have no other properties where you are welcome."

"I will go to your father and throw myself on his mercy. Let him know what kind of son he has raised."

"You won't." But it was too late; the desperation was in his voice. He heard it; she heard it. She turned on her heel and exited through the door farthest from him.

He was halfway through the door after her when he heard his butler's, "Sir?"

He stopped. "What is it?"

The butler's eyes studiously avoided the sofa, in a way which proclaimed he could plainly see it.

"Another visitor, sir. His card." This time, there was a tray. Tate huffed his way over to pick it up. *O'Brien. Who the hell's that?*

Chapter 41

Rafferty

Eleven months after his fight with death, and Lennán could finally walk out to the creek that flowed through their neighborhood and back without fearing a crash. He sat on the retaining wall of the cemetery to listen to the rill burble past, thinking.

He had not written his brother in America, though he had the address. Or rather, he had not *sent* anything. One draft weighed down with too much guilt, another did not acknowledge their shared troubles. All of them, whether crumpled up in the fire or sitting in his brain, felt inadequate. He shouldn't need to look to his children for example, but there they were.

Christopher was finally doing well with his wife and family, running a tavern. Ruarí, in the same business but at the other end of it, ran a grog shop, alone. He had come to his father once for money, but generally they kept apart. Different priests, different neighborhoods. They might have had politics to agree on, but then Lennán had never wanted to raise his head above the crowd for that, after his brothers were scattered.

Then there was Alís, safely married to a teacher and moved to Dublin. She'd had some disappointments, but now had a healthy child, and he'd even been over to see to the wetting of the baby's head two years ago. It had been both a heart-break and a pleasure to set foot on Irish soil again, after more than thirty years. *Do I tell my brother about that in a letter?*

And Orla: the only one to step across the lines to the terrorizers' side. He had been afraid for her, then resentful, and finally, he had grieved for her. With her always on the move about the country with that fool husband, it was like a death. But now she had come back, and had all this muddle over finances the fool husband had left. *Have done with it,* he would have told her, if she'd asked, which she hadn't.

But she had shown him her letter.

It was like her. Neither of them had polish when it came to words, but she had managed sincerity and more: some subtlety of hope and welcome was in her words. He would wait to see Murchadh's reply to her.

A bit of commotion from the birds in the trees made him look up behind him. A train of mourners was winding its way toward a tree near the top of the hill: a great willow. He remembered running from the tree to the church when his children had been young enough to play. A priest was reading out a passage, the rhythm almost distinct enough for Lennán to recognize. He stopped craning his neck and turned back to the shadowed water.

Lennán watched the rill curl by, his eye caught at the places where ripples broke the surface and showed the presence of boulders below. *Not too late,* he thought, and stayed a bit longer.

Chapter 42

O'Brien

Time was running out for O'Brien in Glasgow; he was needed back in London. And so he paid a visit to a very powerful man, albeit a known bully.

As he stood in the foyer of Tate's luxuriously appointed home, he thought of the connections that tethered Widow Smith to this household. A wife who had pointed the finger at her friend, perhaps in order to secure a marriage? *Right bollocks thing to do, that.* And the man himself had schemed to pay his debts by harming Mrs. Smith. He didn't want to leave him alive, when he thought of it that way.

After several minutes' waiting, O'Brien identified the out-of-place smell taunting his nose: caramel. His mouth crooked in irony at the sweet smell clinging to such a foul man. Good to know Tate still frequented his father's factories.

Finally, the butler returned and conducted him to an empty office. Before O'Brien hatched any devious thoughts of search and seizure, the man of the house strode in, stopping in the doorway. He raked a gaze over O'Brien's clothing and shoes.

"Who are you?"

I must not look worth the civilities. "I sent in my card—"

"It is an exceedingly bad time to be thrusting yourself on my acquaintance, so tell me what business brings you here. Now."

O'Brien pushed his eyebrows up at this rudeness.

"My business, my man..." His words curled at the edges with ire. "Here's how it is. You've put a target on the back of a woman. An innocent woman! And a well-connected friend."

Tate sneered.

"And between her connections, we've pieced together your weaknesses, Tate. Your family may be wealthy, but you've built your house on sand. Owing money and squeezing tenants. Hiding losses and cheating the inspectors." He clucked his tongue like a disappointed schoolmaster. "And that's going to stop."

Introducing his debts had wiped the smirk off his face, but no recognition yet lit him up. O'Brien went in for the kill.

"Because the friends that know about all this include a bleedin' pack of journalists. With Glasgow and London papers happy to print such a story, you'd be hard-pressed to believe the things you've got up to—"

"That's enough."

"I agree. You're going to leave here. Sell this place and its furnishings, if it's not mortgaged already. And take that lovely adder wife of yours to the Continent. You'll be safe there," he finished on a chilling whisper. And by the look on Tate's face, he'd left him with enough detail to scare him into action.

He left without waiting for the butler.

In London, O'Brien was free to be his more ruthless self: demanding to be seen by officials, firing off editorials to bosses, taking a hard line with Members of Parliament when they allowed questions from the press. He was exhausted after several weeks of this, but didn't mention it in his letter to McNary. No matter; the fight demanded all his strength.

His latest meeting, on a June morning with Mr. Lovett, was going well. Lovett seemed to know every subject and have plans for harnessing the power of the new Parliament to effect progress.

"You're going by Bronterre, now, is it?" he asked as they took a pause for fresh coffee.

"Yes, I thought it would help people remember an Irish name," O'Brien said, a little sheepish. Lovett swept on with more grand plans, heedless of his companion's discomfort.

"Fine. But what of your statement about slaves living a happier life than the laborers in England, James? We can not have that on the books, not with the pamphlet coming out from Sturge. Have you read it?"

"I have the gist." In fact, he had given Orla his copy of the report, a pamphlet about the terrible conditions present in the West Indies.

"We do not advance by comparison with others in terrible circumstances—at least not if we question the seriousness of either plight. I would rather see the slaves—"

"Former slaves," O'Brien corrected.

"Right—former slaves brought into the fold as free laborers whose conditions improve right along ours. And how to do it? Information! Campaigns! Pamphlets. Speakers. You could go," he insisted, and O'Brien was listening to the melodious exhortation so well he didn't realize it ended for a moment.

"Me!"

"Harney could also go. But not until this apprentice program is abolished as well. The rebellions make it dangerous for anyone new, anyone unknown. That is what Sturge says to me in his letter, at any rate."

He was dumbfounded. O'Brien had worked for Radical newspapers for years now, exhausted himself organizing, investigating, insisting on rights—and now they wanted to sacrifice him to the slavery cause?

"That is seven more years," he said slowly. "What is your plan in the meantime?"

"There is no meantime, man. It is all, now! Every man for every man, and our demands will be easy boons to grant, with this wave that is taking Parliament—"

"William, we do not know that. We can not count on it. You know the power of the manufacturers, the monstrous middle classes. God forbid, the aristocracy—"

"But they have suffered the first blow, James!"

"Yes, and like a noxious weed, it was not aimed at the root, so it will grow back higher and faster! Like a hurt animal, it will attack more viciously!" O'Brien was breathing heavily, his heart hammering. He always felt passionately about his causes, but he hadn't talked himself out of breath in a fair while.

There was a pause. Lovett sipped his cooling coffee.

"Have you lost confidence? Or is it a weakness you see?"

Or both, thought O'Brien. But he merely shook his head. His companion sighed.

"It is a worthy goal, William. Of course, a vote for every man and rights in his work—it is the dignity we fight for. Only I don't want us painting too rosy a picture and men getting discouraged."

Lovett cocked an eyebrow, clearly challenging whether he had not already arrived there himself.

"It will be a long, bloody battle. It's almost as if I can see it. Like massed hordes, with ghostly banners and mounted chargers. God, it is like the mass of us have neither shield nor helmet, and we're taunting the soldiers to run us through." His voice was hoarse, and though it wasn't his overall confidence that was dampened, he was feeling quite hopeless in this moment of his vision. In fact, it was a memory of his come back: one dark morning in Ireland when the people had stood, and been run clean over.

"They can't do it to everyone," Lovett said gently. "So we must merely dodge and parry between every thrust of our pen."

O'Brien gave his friend a weak smile and thought of Orla. She had stayed at her home for several days after being knocked down, even though they didn't know she'd be safe there. She'd made a plan, sent her secret plans to her generals in the rear guard and the flank, and they'd turned the tide for her, so it seemed. *Dodge. Parry. Thrust.*

O'Brien gave a curt nod, and they went over Lovett's plans for a manifesto.

Chapter 43

Orla

At last, the fall harvests coming in brought the purchase of wheat within reach, and the women in the region were able to make bread for their families, along with the beans, peas, oats, and other local stores. Their small group was able to step back their ambitious food relief efforts, and Amelia came to speak with Orla about the future.

"Of course I belong with my order, unless I'm sent on a specific errand or assignment," she was saying. Orla served her a warm scone and pushed the butter dish closer.

"I am very glad the sisters saw fit to respond to the call from Mr. McNary. But you are allowed to correspond? It's not a—a…"

"Cloister? No. We are a working convent, mainly in the poor lanes, like the work I did here. And yes, I will certainly write. I can't claim to be an entertaining correspondent, but I'm regular." Orla smiled wistfully, her heart hurting for this daughter of a man who felt little tie to his own.

"Your father wrote back." Her cousin's quick intake of breath made her proceed slowly. "He was curious about how my father was doing." She gave Amelia a wry grin. "Of course I didn't give him too many details; I told him to write to him directly."

Amelia laughed brokenly. Orla clasped her hand.

"He has a family there, you told us. And he told me about them, a little. He seems well settled there."

"That he does," she agreed quietly.

"You can have mine," Orla said with a spark of mischief. Amelia snorted, then sobered.

"Aye. It would be good to stay close now. And Fergal in Australia..." she sighed. "I'd have no idea how to find him in the prison lists, would you?"

Orla squinted. "Not specifically, but I know where to start."

Amelia squeezed her hand, then released it to take a bite of scone. "This is really nice. The currants, and just a touch of... something sweeter."

Smiling broadly, Orla answered, "That is my niece's handiwork! I've no idea, but she's becoming a wizard in the kitchen, and likes to visit when she can get away from tavern chores."

They talked of family, and meetings soon to come, and ended with promises of sharing news and a visit to be returned. Orla was well happy to gain a cousin.

"Oh, no, the harvests haven't changed the wages at all. They changed prices of food stuffs, but not wages, so the factory workers do better, but the agricultural laborers are just as badly off as before. They've set us against each other."

Mr. Lovett was a guest at the monthly meeting of journalists. One of the assembled raised a hand to ask, "So how do they get to be on the same side against the landowners, professor?"

Lovett quirked his lips briefly at the sobriquet. "Communication, Mr. Gamble! Articles, pamphlets, distribution, meetings, sermons—"

Someone let out a disbelieving guffaw.

"I'm serious! What do you think the great speakers in the field are but preachers of the Word of God in economic terms?"

A stunned silence as the men, and Orla, took in that statement.

"Forget the differences of religion for a moment. What we are divided by is *control*. The rich control the prices that affect our survival, the farmers' and the workers'. Think! The price of bread doesn't fall from the sky; neither does the system to make it easier or harder to get produce to market, to get children to a school of higher education, or to have access to credit."

He sent a significant look in Orla's direction. She bristled, and felt singled out. *James must have told him my story.* When she sought O'Brien's gaze, it was focused on the table; he was trying hard to add something to Lovett's argument, she thought.

Another journalist asked about the levers of power, and how they were to be pressed to make changes to benefit the working classes. He did not look at her, but Orla blushed, conscious of how she had two friends who had done her great service, pressing on those levers. *Connections.* If only she had a more extensive web of connections. Then she looked at the journalists assembled.

All of them from elsewhere. All of them educated at established colleges or universities. All of them working for multiple newspapers over years and years.

As she had been watching O'Brien, trying to work out what gears his mind was winding, her train of thought was interrupted by him.

"What has you looking so radiantly positive, Mrs. Smith?"

All heads swiveled toward her. Disconcerted, Orla opened her mouth but hesitated. Mr. Lovett smiled knowingly; perhaps he knew what had crossed her mind?

"Those things Mr. Lovett mentions, vegetables getting to market, children going to school, a lone widow having access to credit—these are all possible if you have connections. People make exceptions for personal ties. Not only the rich. So... the people you grew up with—anyone know a shopkeeper?"

Several hands went skeptically up.

"The men you went to school with—any of them work at a bank?"

A few other hands.

"The editors who pass you work—any of them have pet causes? Or know tutors who could prepare a student for an exam?"

She'd made her point. Hands came down.

"We asked for help for the workers who might have had to strike in the spring, and we got it," said McNary, continuing her theme. "And the entire fight will consist of us helping each other survive, independent of the bribery and temptation from the rich. We mustn't let them divide us. Rights are what we want, not privileges, eh?"

It was a more roused McNary than she'd seen before: his face was animated.

"The Reform candidates are in and doing their part. We have to keep the presses on the job now, too. We keep pushing."

Chapter 44

Olive

Quarter Day Fair and Harvest Day festivities were over. The trees were burnished with gold, starting to litter the lanes and fields with crackling skeletons. Olive was old enough to take a ride from the dairy man going west until the Pollok Estate, then walk the three miles over field to Crookston to see her aunt.

Olive had grown up knowing her father had siblings, but had not met any of them until last year. Up til then it had only been her mother's brothers and her grandfather Rafferty, who wasn't all that fun to visit. But he loved them well, she understood.

When she'd been confronted with an aunt, who lived less than ten miles away, she'd felt strangely angry at her for showing up with no warning. Olive did not like surprises. Then she realized she wasn't angry at Aunt Smith, but at her own father for not telling her. Then she'd become very curious.

An intrigue! With her very own aunt! That had been thrilling, indeed. Olive wondered if there would be more excitement in her aunt's future. She did love being helpful, and since her parents and siblings seemed so safe and ordinary, she rather thought she'd insinuate herself over in this direction and see what she could learn.

And she had written in advance, like a proper grown-up, to say she was coming. She felt very mature indeed, with her new drawers and proper stays, as she strode by the houses of Crookston village. She wished one old woman good morning, and was similarly saluted. When she arrived at her aunt's cottage, however, apprehension climbed up her skin once again.

"Olive! Come in."

The smile was strained, she could tell. She waited til they were inside and seated before asking.

"What's wrong?" Looking around she could see the sturdy table was covered in newspapers, as well as the sofa and chairs.

"Where's Lev?" Olive had met the feline when she stayed over last month and warmed to him immediately.

Still, her aunt didn't answer. Olive cast about for an explanation and her eye caught on one of the newsprint pages. She wasn't a great reader, but she could recognize common words. The word 'radical' was repeated several times, and though she could sound it out, she had no idea what it meant. She bit her lip and decided to wait for an explanation.

"Our friend Lev is having a little trouble with his legs, Olive. He leapt in the window all right yesterday evening but then his back legs started going different directions and he—he got a little panicked. I've—I've wrapped him up tight in a blanket and he's resting. I hope it's over, but I don't think it's the sort of thing one gets better from. I'm just sad he's gotten old so quickly, when we'd just become such good companions." She smiled sadly.

"It's old age, then?"

"Well, probably not. It may be a disease—he does go outdoors and I'm sure he gets into all sorts of questionable substances—but whatever it is, I don't want him to feel panic like that."

Olive was silent a moment in respect for her aunt's feelings, but then asked about the newspapers.

"Oh, I was looking for mention of people who might be good allies—leaders in the fight for the right to dignity and rest." She'd brightened right up, so Olive encouraged her to keep talking by volunteering some information.

"I've finished with the school, the one I pointed out to you down the road."

"Well, now; how did you like it?"

Olive shrugged a shoulder. "The maths were all right, but I couldn't see the use of knowing what ancient philosopher said what, and which battle with the Huns was what year."

"Fair enough, so no to rhetoric and history. Why were the maths all right?"

"Because I could see I'd need to know it, to help tot up the accounts at the tavern, like Ma does now."

"You think you'll succeed to the post?"

Olive blushed. "I dunno, I suppose I'd be helping out Ma, or…maybe marrying someone else who had a similar place or shop."

"Ah," replied her aunt. "So you want to do what your parents do?"

"It wouldn't be the worst," Olive replied, having heard that exact refrain many times. Her aunt smiled as if she heard its echo too.

"Definitely not the worst. But of your schoolfellows, what types of work did their parents do? What subjects did they take up?"

"Well…my friend Jenny's parents run a mercer shop. And Andrew's family have a boarding house. I had a wine merchant's twin sons in class for a few years. Some of the mothers went out to clean. One o' them took in laundry," she said in a whisper.

"And is that the worst?"

"Well, no…it's honest, but…Ma says it's often the dishonest women that do it," she said in another half-whisper.

"Laundry is rough work, and no mistake. Strips your skin with lye and steam and roasts your bones when you're bending over the tub and washboard."

Olive could picture it, even all the bother it would be to get fuel to keep the fire going for the water. "Tis why so many of them do it together, I suppose—someone works on the hot water for them and they get through it faster."

"Have you ever seen a washerwoman on her day of rest, Olive?"

The girl thought, but couldn't recollect any memory of it.

"That is because they do not have one. The prices are so low for their services that they need to be at it every day, except for when they need to do their food shop."

Olive made to object then thought better of it. She did not want to seem to be whining. "Why are the prices so low?"

Aunt Smith nodded in approval at the question.

"Because that's all the rich families will pay. They have lots of money and can make their own servants do the work, but they save them the hassle by hiring out. And there are so many women who need money and want it honestly, that they will do this hard work for pennies."

Aunt Smith paused a moment before continuing. "If you feel you need to talk about hard-working women in a whisper, it is because they have been painted as without dignity, and without leisure. We mean to give everyone both things: dignity and leisure."

Olive wondered who 'we' referred to.

"...Men who are miners, children who are sweeps, women who sew, even the Blacks who serve their masters here after gaining their freedom. God gives everyone certain inalienable rights, I've just been reading one of those philosophers say that very thing. Let me see..."

She drew Olive's attention to a book she drew from a shelf, opening to a place marked by a blue silk ribbon. Aunt Smith continued the point with this man Locke's words, and a quarter of an hour later, Olive was nodding and agreeing.

"So, not so pointless after all?" When Olive blushed and looked down, her aunt took a different tone, less teasing, more restrained. "And how did you find your cousin Amelia, Sister St. Clarence?"

"She seemed glad to see us that first supper," she said cautiously. "I only had supper with her one other time, before she left to go back to Manchester. She seemed a bit put off by us, by then. Cold-shouldered. But it could be she was tired before the journey. She doesn't like crowds, she told us."

"No, she had a very bad experience with one when she was young. And what do you mean, put off?"

"Just, not wanting to touch us, not warm, like you."

It was her aunt's turn to blush and shake her head. "Olive, she has had different life experiences—a nun! And I'm sure she's glad to know more of her kin."

"Yes, I suppose. She seems more like Grandfather Rafferty than you do."

Aunt Smith seemed to consider this, and nodded. "I think you're right. It makes me wonder what her father Murchadh was like." She got a faraway glisten in her eyes and dropped the subject. "Well. Would you like to help me with supper?"

Her conscience at rest, Olive enthusiastically assented and they enjoyed a sociable meal together.

Chapter 45

Orla

The frost of the mornings had been too much for Lev, and he'd yowled at Orla one day fierce enough to drop him. He stalked out the open front door, back legs stiff, with his dignity. Orla supposed him to want to choose his own way to submit to Fate, and she couldn't begrudge him that. She did cry that day, though.

The *Bankers' Circular* was still in a churn about the terms for the massive government debt project of repaying the slaveholders, and she was tsking and tutting her way through their declamations when she heard noise outside. Untroubled, she marked her place with a book and went to peek out the window. She saw nothing, but the faint noise was growing; she opened her door.

A faint outline of a crowd was traveling north on the village road, a few taller shadows signaling horses. The noise was of bells and a murmur of song. They were a few hundred yards off, and Orla looked around to see if others had noticed. They had: two other doors framed housewives in aprons, interrupted in the morning chores.

The song—as soon as it was distinguishable, Orla let loose a delighted chuckle. She could see women walking now, their thick shawls joining the men in their dark wool coats. She dashed inside to gather two cups and unstopper a jug of cider. She filled them hastily and carried them outside, posing at the edge of the road to offer them to members of the band.

One of the other onlookers disappeared, following her example. She heard a shout further on in the village. She kept her attention on the leaders as they approached, and the words reached her ears, "In the factory, where I stay…"

"Yes!" she shouted.

One of the men saw her holding the mug and came to take a long sip, as if she were a priest at a Mass. Then a woman passed her, still singing, and nodded. Another man took a grateful sip, wiping his chin on a sleeve. Orla felt filled with hope from the show of solidarity, at the feeling that they would be heard, in the capital, and the voices of power forced to listen.

She wished her niece was here for this.

Dear Olive,

Your father recently told me that your name made him think of me, when I was far away in the years we were apart. And so, as women with 'O' names, a sort of clandestine affinity has existed between us. I am so glad, and honored, to be a holder of your confidences.

Our conversation about schooling made me think deeply about the subject on a larger scale. We should talk about this next time we are together. Maybe we will even invite others into our confidence to do so? I know a certain circle of seamstresses has been debating the value of a union in their ranks, and might be very curious to know about what you've learnt in schools they never got to attend. Neither did I, come to that!

I know your excellent mother and father will talk to you of these things as well, but I am glad to put my oar in, and help you row out from shore, as it were. I was quite young when I left my family to work, only twelve years. It was six years as maid-of-all-work before I was married to my Robert, my husband. I know you don't think of domestic service as your future, but I wish you not to be embarrassed by any profession that is honest. I would hope you would not have to whisper that your aunt was a maid when you speak long after I am gone.

I helped people as a curate's, and then a minister's, wife, and I am finding another way to do so as a widow, one in which I myself benefit by learning more about the world. I hope you have the curiosity to seek out knowledge and the security to consider matters fairly, without fear of shame. Women can be so afraid of shame that they can become monsters to one another, and that helps no one, unless it be those men who hate women.

I am wandering from my point, which is to say, I bless your name and hold your friendship close to my heart. Let us look forward to 1835 with joy and anticipation! Yours truly,

Aunt Smith

Chapter 46

"My 'girls?' Please, Bronterre, don't call them that. It's…"

"Debasing," supplied Louise. She sat at Orla's right hand, one of three ladies in a room full of men. McNary stood by the wall, either a lookout or a disciplinarian overseeing the meeting's activities.

"Yes, belittling. We are not a flock of hens. Simply acknowledge another committee working on an aspect of the Charter demands. Equal." She eyed her friend, who stood at his place opposite her.

"Fine, fine. You win." He cleared his throat to address the other men. "Apologies, withdrawn. Now, for Miss Esther's report?"

The woman from Lord Rosebery's estate stood as well, and Orla was pleased to see it was with a new confidence. Not an apology or a stammer in sight. She had certainly improved her delivery in the past eight months of practice, Orla thought approvingly. She headed a separate committee that was gathering facts on the material situation for the agricultural laborers, both in work in the rural areas and out of work, on relief.

"Let me add my voice to the congratulations for the Charter committee," Esther began, nodding her head in the direction of one of the male journalists. "And I am glad to hear of Mr. Lovett's work progressing in London. Now, as for our figures," and she read from her paper, citing rents and budgets and rates and assessments. Interested looks from the men, the scratching of their pens, and Orla breathed a deep sigh of vindication. They had also improved in the past eight months. Accustomed to her presence, they had initially balked at letting a woman of color into the room for these strategic discussions, until she'd reminded them that those who had a stake in the outcomes deserved a voice in the proceedings. Their own principles could not be shouted down.

Another balked at the suggestion she be able to form a committee of work. But now: look at them! Orla glanced at her niece, who was treating it all as normal. She wondered if she took any of this attitude home, where she still lived with her parents and sister.

"We recommend," Esther was concluding, "Mr. Kelly's policy of small meetings to continue, and that the potential leaders we identified be asked to organize around the campaigns to pay Members a salary and to have districts of equal size, as those are the causes they could speak most plainly to and most passionately on, with their brother and sister workers."

Esther raised her brows in Orla's direction.

"Excellent work, thank you, Esther."

After calling her Miss Primrose for some time, Esther had approached her with the request not to use her employer's name for her surname. She still used it for legal requirements, but she said she did not wish to use it when doing work that mattered, like the bank for the workers and the Charter for electoral reform.

"I'd like my own name to be how I'm remembered in this circle," she had said. Orla's hand touched her own ribcage, the feeling of power reclaimed echoing in her own belly.

The bank was doing well for them, and they had embarked on this new path together with their friends, of changing the system that kept them powerless. It was the only way.

On a day much later, a day filled with crushing disappointment, Orla sat in a rented room in the capital and sobbed. She had traveled to London with McNary on one of the new trains, worried but hopeful for at least some progress. They had been crushed, their crowds denied, their ideas dismissed.

All our work, ran the moaning chorus in her head. *All that work.*

She didn't know London well, but she had arranged to meet her cousin there. Sister St. Clarence—Amelia—was eager to see her, not as intimately bound up with the details of the campaign. Amelia had focused more on the relief efforts, following the plight of the workers only when it meant actual change in their needs and thus something she could address directly with food or medicine or blankets. Orla knew she had to stop crying and wash her face. With an immense act of will, she straightened her back and shakily stood. Seeing the tremble in her hands she didn't pick up the pitcher of water but dipped her hands in, covering her face and slowing her hitched breathing.

She tidied herself and went out. Amelia looked up at her entrance to the tea room, all smiles, but her expression quickly changed when Orla approached.

"What is it? Who's died?"

"Nobody," Orla answered shortly, though it had been a close thing, when a soldier restrained one of their marchers a little too fervently. Michael was in the hospital for the night with a dislocated or broken arm. *The knife edge*, Orla thought.

"Well, then, why is your face all stormy?"

"Stormy…? We've lost." She felt baffled by the confused look on her cousin's face. "Amelia, the Commons closed debate on our Charter before anyone could comment. The speaker was mobbed. The session continued with all other business like it was nothing."

"Do they allow women to observe?"

"No, but—"

"Then you didn't see yourself? How do you know?"

"Multiple members of the committee told me the same thing. After three, I stopped listening."

"Ah. Three does seem like decent corroboration."

Orla let a moment's silence go by before urging herself to do her duty to family anyway and ask about Amelia's situation.

"How have you found London? You've been here with the new order, what, four months now?"

"Oh, yes! It is fine work. I never thought of myself as a schooling type of religious, but these children are very clever, and so good-hearted. I think I am much more needed here than I was in Manchester or Liverpool. If Mother Abigail can see her way to transferring me, I think I'll be happier here as well." She beamed.

Orla gave a watery smile, but felt the lump in her throat threaten to transform itself into a flood.

"You know, Orla, I was eager to come to you today because I am in a good situation, yes, but also I've had good news."

"Oh, yes?" Orla mustered interest.

"Our uncle Fergal who was sent off to the penal colonies—he made his way back to Ireland." Orla's whole body jerked to attention. "I'm just after hearing from a woman in the new order that she knew his wife, what do you think of that!"

"And how," Orla said, trying to follow, "did a woman in your convent know a woman in Australia?"

"She said they married in Australia and emigrated back. She met the wife in Ireland, when she was chorister to a church—"

"Where are they now, Amelia?" Her voice came out with a desperate rasp. She winced as she waited for the information.

"Oh, the wife died some time ago, but they lived in Wicklow, somewhere…"

"County or City?"

"I'm sure we didn't get to the particulars, but she thought the husband and children would have stayed put. Not keen on travel, sure they weren't."

Orla slowed down her charging-ahead heart long enough to try to think reasonably. "How did you ever come to discover that you both knew the same man?"

"Oh, simple. She asked about my name, I told her. She told me about this woman, and I asked her all she could remember. It wasn't much, but she did write down the church they went to. It'll have their children's baptisms."

Orla smiled wide. "You're right! Well done. Well done, that's one step closer to finding another branch of our family. It seems I may have stumbled a bit in my mission today, but you brought me back to what's important, Amelia."

"You never know which connection will bring you closer to your goal. Or which battle will be crucial to win," Amelia said. Orla nodded, glad to claw back one victory from the day.

Did you enjoy this book?

Please consider posting a review on any site where you go to look for them yourself.

Reviews like yours help the book find its way to the hands of new readers! This helps self-published authors like me gain readers online and through word-of-mouth networks. You are cordially invited to visit my author website at www.margaretpinard.com and follow along on the Patreon blog at bit.ly/patreon_mp4 for news, events, and giveaways.

My eternal thanks for your time, attention, and encouragement.

Author's Note

This is the last piece to be tackled for this novel, but one I've thought about since the beginning. What do readers expect when it comes to historical fiction? When does possibility take on the aspect of reality, and is there a responsibility to notify the reader of the transition?

As a ravenous reader of historical fiction myself, I love immersing myself in the past precisely because it has the potential to teach me about the past, that foreign country. In fact, I have learned about many pasts, and many foreign countries in this way. I may have made a few mistakes over the years, assuming that something I read was the truth when it was artistic license. The one most imprinted on my memory was believing the musical style choices in *Joseph and the Amazing Technicolor Dreamcoat* actually indicated that the sons of Jacob lived in France, which led to a very embarrassing moment in 7th grade social studies. But I've learned that lesson: always confirm the fact when you return to reality!

And that's what an author's note should do, in my opinion. So who are the people in the novel with some roots in reality? I have taken the most liberties with James Bronterre O'Brien, an Irish journalist who was a towering figure in the Chartism movement. Very little of his personal life is known, so before he presumably married and had children, I extended his frequent trips throughout the Midlands and the North to Glasgow and made him a friend to Orla.

Next are Mr. James Ewing, Mr. William Lovett, Archibald Primrose, Lord Dalmeny, all of whom appear briefly on the page and serve as messengers for the cause they fought for in real life. Ewing was an M.P. for Glasgow, and an influential member of the West Indian lobby, campaigning for continued slavery in the colonies. Incidentally, his cousin was Rev. Ralph Wardlaw, an ardent abolitionist. Lovett, a cabinet-maker, absorbed Liberal teachings early and went on to become involved in co-operative societies, trades unions, and the London Working Men's Association before becoming a powerful organizing voice for the Chartists. I've imagined a strategic conversation for Lovett and O'Brien that plants the seeds for their later Chartist battles, which you may just see in a sequel. And Lord Dalmeny was a convenient Whig politician from the area who later married a woman historian! So I made him a good, progressive, enabling sort of chap.

And finally, there are those names mentioned but not present in the story, that I drew from history. Oswald, Stevenson, and Co. was an actual firm run by two Oswald brothers and two Stevenson brothers, dealing in mercantile transactions in cottons and yarns. Oswald also formed part of Glasgow Bank's early founders.

Oswald was one of the leading supporters of the movement that led to the Reform Act of 1832, and became one of the first M.P.'s elected after it passed. He was a Member during the time frame for this novel, in fact, and there is nothing to indicate his firm swindled business partners.

There is brief mention of a Mr. Snow, a doctor with a theory about disease communication. This connection of O'Brien's is named for the man known for discovering the source of a cholera outbreak in London almost two decades later (John Snow). But the idea to include a doctor-philanthropist in the cast was inspired by the history of the 'three Ayrshire toons' I visited, where Dr. Alexander McFadzean had worked for and among the poor. He was highly regarded enough that at his death the public erected a monument on Castle Hill in Ardrossan. In order to contribute in my own small way to his memory, I let him inspire an off-page character.

The publication written by Joseph Sturge is, in fact, real (*Narrative of Events since the First of August 1834*), but I took the fictional liberty of having it published two years earlier than it actually was, so that I could have his reporting move my characters to a common cause. He was an advocate for radical electoral reform and abolition, and the pamphlet I refer to was an account of his travels to the West Indies to ascertain the state of the transitional 'apprenticeship' system. Since this was nothing more than extended slavery, he fought for and helped achieve its early repeal by publishing its horrors. Full abolition was realized first by Trinidad, two years before Parliament had planned for the apprenticeships to be dissolved.

This is the first time I've woven so many actual historical characters into a novel, and I hope to do more in the sequels, highlighting the brave souls who looked into the injustices of their time and took what actions they could to alter history. My hope is that their presence inspires people today to learn and change our histories, too.

Acknowledgements

Orla Rafferty is my first novel to be published since the pandemic and all its life changes descended in 2019. It has been a twisty, mountainous ride. The fact that this novel has risen from the bottom of the heap to see the light of day is due in no small part to the many folks who have stoked the fires of curiosity and applied the balm of encouragement.

Thank you to my Patrons who have seen me through four years of much dithering and stochastic research! I love sending your book mail, I enjoyed *most* of the books for book club, and I have benefited myself from sharing my in-process thoughts on the blog. Special shout-outs to Skye Winter for talking me off a website ledge and to Emma Bennet for clutch last-minute advice.

Thank you to Christie Stratos, my editor, whose Victorian flair made her such a perfect match. Thank you to my beta readers Alison and Sarah who provided feedback as only engaged readers and encouraging friends can. Thank you to Booktube friends met and sprinted with along the way, who helped me keep me on task.

Thank you to all those who helped me during my research journeys, including Multnomah County Library, the Library of Congress's Ask A Reference Librarian program, the North Ayrshire Heritage Centre, and the Mitchell Library's City Archives in Glasgow. All these information system professionals are indispensable to our investigations into history, without which we could have no context for how to shape our future.

About the Author

Margaret Pinard is a soul from the 19th century who finds it easiest to disguise herself by drinking tea, writing historical fiction, and popping off to the British Isles for 'research.' She has published six novels and one collection of short stories. Her historical fiction work includes the *Remnants* trilogy which follows the MacLean family from 1820s Scotland to Canada and beyond, highlighting the immigrant experience. Margaret has co-founded an indie book festival, helped run a writing conference, and is a firm ally of independent bookstores. She splits her time between Portland, OR and San Luis Obispo, CA.

Printed in the USA
CPSIA information can be obtained
at www.ICGtesting.com
CBHW031053011224
18274CB00040B/468